LOCKWOOD COVEN BOOK ONE

HER GHOSTLY EMBRACE

COLETTE RIVERA

Edited by Hummingbird Editing

Proofreading by CJ Editing

Cover art by Neon Jess

ISBN

Print: 978-1-991284-17-4

Kindle: 978-1-991284-18-1

AUTHOR'S NOTE

Dear reader,

This book deals with adult themes and is intended for mature audiences. The following is an outline of possible triggers and general content warnings. Please look after yourself and take care.

Content Guidance and Trigger Warnings (may contain spoilers to the mystery elements of the story):

Sexual content: intended for mature audiences.

Character with an undiagnosed, fictional illness. Ablism from side characters directed at this character. Some instances of internalized ablism.

Main character forced into a betrothal against their will.

Misogyny.

Gaslighting.

Abusive family dynamics.

Mention of suicide in reference to what others might think happened to the character that turns into a ghost: The other witches in the Thornfield Coven might think Aurora killed herself because, from the outside, her "death" may look like a suicide by magic. To be clear, Aurora does *not* commit suicide or have suicidal thoughts. She isn't dead (as outlined in the book description). She casts a spell to separate her soul from her body with the intention of living through it. However, she acknowledges the risk that the magic could fail and she could die accidentally. She is in a place where she is willing to take this risk to save herself from her situation, and while not being the same as suicidal ideation, this is still a dark place for the character to be.

Main character being stalked/followed on-page by an antagonist.

Murder: on and off page. Antagonists killed on page. Repeated discussion of a man (antagonist) who had his wife killed. It later becomes clear that he killed his wife himself.

Witches who worship Satan.

Characters bound by magic against their will.

Fantasy violence. Blood magic. Blood-drinking vampires.

Mind control. Character's memories magically altered without their consent. Character forced by magic to commit violent acts against their will.

Physical violence: fights between antagonists and protagonists.

Firearms used on-page.

Car accident resulting in fatalities with a child in the car (child survives).

Torture on-page but not described in detail.

Child witnessing extreme violence.

Fire: burning of property, structures, and forest land, as well as mention of wildfires/forest fires. A building with people inside catches fire after an explosion. Person (antagonist) burned by magical means, then set on fire.

Main character buried alive. Grave digging.

LOCKWOOD COVEN BOOK ONE

HER GHOSTLY EMBRACE

COLETTE RIVERA

ONE

GIA

Everything unraveled the day Gianna Balzano found out her Aunt Susan died. First of all, she didn't have an Aunt Susan.

"Yes, you do," said the man on the phone. "I can explain. She was related to you by blood on your father's side—"

Gia spoke over him. "Sorry. You've got the wrong number." She scrubbed a hand over her face, more concerned with her killer headache than anything this guy had to say. Dealing with bullheaded arrogance was a waste of what little energy she had.

As if she weren't aware her father had no siblings.

"I'm not mistaken," the man said with careful patience. "You're exactly who I need to speak to, Miss Balzano. Susan Lockwood was very clear in her final wishes. I'm sorry to bring you news of her passing, especially if this is the first—"

"No, you listen. I don't have any aunts or uncles." How dare he lie about someone's death, offering pretend condolences? Gia sat upright in bed, and her head throbbed, vision tunneling for a split second. "How did you even get this number?"

Whoever the hell this guy was, he'd called her private cellphone. Very few people had Gia's number, and none of them would hand it out. They knew better than to risk the consequences.

Like the rest of her family, none of Gia's personal contact details were publicly available, and she wasn't involved in the Balzanos' legitimate businesses, so no one could have found her that way. But the man on the phone knew she was a Balzano, meaning he had an angle. Everyone surrounding her family had an angle. Ambitions. Some sort of scheme.

"Gianna," the man said, his voice turning tender even as it betrayed a hint of steel. "I'm not talking about your father, Franco, I'm talking about Jeffrey. Your biological—"

Gia hung up.

Her hands shook as she blocked the number, and she couldn't tell if it was from anger or the sheer force of her headache. Probably the headache. Weirdos trying to get to her family through her wasn't exactly new. It had just been a while since she'd dealt with anyone like this.

Gia turned off her phone and lay down, pulling the blankets over her. She'd had one of her episodes last night and needed rest.

With a sigh, she pulled a small bottle from her nightstand drawer, fished out a pill, and swallowed it with water. She closed her eyes and waited for it to kick in.

Gia's migraines were of a rare intensity and often led to blackouts in her memory. Her triggers were variable and hard to predict, often leaving managing the aftermath of a headache as her only course of action. After what happened last night, she'd be exhausted and jittery for the rest of the day at least. Overexertion wouldn't do her any favors.

As happened far too frequently, Gia couldn't remember anything after last night's migraine had set in. Salvator had said she'd retreated to her room and slept, so at least she hadn't passed out in the library or somewhere else embarrassingly public, like the time he'd found her slumped at the kitchen table.

Gia strained to remember going to her room. All she could recall was walking through the south wing of the house, past the library and her father's office, on her way to the home gym.

So much for her plans to get on the exercise bike.

Eventually, the pill kicked in and her head cleared. She should tell Salvator about the strange phone call so he could look into it, but again, that required energy.

Gia rolled over and clutched a pillow. *Susan Lockwood.* There was something familiar in the name now that Gia wasn't so distracted by pain and the presumptuous nature of the man on the phone. Lockwood wasn't a common surname as far as Gia was aware. Where had she heard it? Maybe she'd read it in a book.

She fell into a half-doze as her mind ran in circles around the name.

Lockwood...

Gia's tired eyes flew open, and she froze. Lockwood wasn't the only familiar name the man had mentioned. *Jeffrey.* The mysterious Susan's brother, Jeffrey Lockwood.

That's the name of the man who tried to kidnap me.

Gia's heart pounded, but for once, her head gave her no trouble. An old memory surfaced, one Gia had pushed away for years. A sensation like a scratching fingernail dragged down her spine, and the smell of pine trees hit her out of nowhere. She'd been small, only five, on a day out at the park with her nanny and then...a feeling of dread. That was it.

It wasn't much of a memory, but who could blame her for repressing a day that had started with an attempted kidnapping and ended with something far worse?

Gia tried to bring up other details, but couldn't. The only

thing that rang clear was the name 'Jeffrey Lockwood' as it echoed through the cavernous halls of her mind.

Was she remembering correctly?

Gia recalled the story of that fateful day more than the actual event. Not that her family ever talked about it now.

According to the stories Gia had been told, she'd been abducted by a man at the park, and when her mother found out, she'd hunted the kidnapper down to rescue her. The kidnapper and her mother had both died in the resulting fight. Luckily, Salvator had been there as backup, along with some of her father's other men. They'd rescued Gia and brought her home.

Gia hadn't thought about any of this in a while, and guilt immediately filled her. When you were the daughter of a crime boss, you became desensitized to a certain amount of violence, but that wasn't why she'd done her best to never revisit this subject. She hardly remembered her mother, and the pain of losing her had only been made worse by the rest of her family's determination to act like it had never happened.

Franco Balzano hadn't run Ashton Lakes then, and he hadn't wanted to talk about what happened—it must have been painful—but he'd indulged Gia more when she was little and answered her questions. To a point.

Surely she had the man's name wrong. This subject had been closed for a long time. No one had mentioned Letti Balzano in any real capacity since Gia was about ten. Could she really expect to remember what her father had told her fifteen or more years ago?

Now she considered it, Gia didn't actually remember her father telling her who had taken her and killed her mother. Not by name. She'd heard the name 'Jeffrey Lockwood' murmured between her father and his men while she'd been crouching outside his office door after they'd moved into the big house.

She'd been a terrible little spy as a child, but of all the things she'd overheard, this stuck out, and for some reason, she was convinced it had to do with that horrible day at the park.

But why the hell was someone calling and claiming the man's sister was her *aunt*?

Gia turned her phone on. A voicemail from a restricted number popped up. She ignored it and called her brother.

He picked up after two rings. "Hey, sis," Marc drawled. "How are you feeling? Okay?"

So he'd heard about her latest episode. "I'm fine."

"You don't have to pretend with me, G. Want me to bring you anything? I'll be at the house in about an hour."

He wasn't home? Gia had called because she didn't feel up to crossing the sprawling estate to her brother's room. "What are you doing?"

Marc sighed. "Nothing. Supervising. You know. Want something from Antonio's? It's on my way, and I'm guessing you haven't had lunch."

Gia gritted her teeth.

She didn't understand why her brother and father half-heartedly shielded her from the less savory parts of the family business. *Supervising.* She knew who the Balzano family was and what they did. The drugs. The guns. The money. The people who disappeared. Gia had no choice but to be a part of organized crime, even if she was spared from getting her hands dirty.

So why the lackluster attempts to keep her in the dark?

Were they playing along with her disinterest? Gia wasn't proud to be a Balzano. She had no interest in her family's power and didn't condone what they did, but she was helpless to stop any of it. People who disagreed with her father died. There was no leaving the family unless you were zipped in a body bag.

Gia's stomach turned. "Yeah, sounds good, Marc. See you soon." She hung up.

In a body bag. Like her mother.

Gia shook her head. Why was she thinking about it like that? Her mother hadn't tried to leave. The kidnapper had killed her.

The man her mysterious caller claimed was her biological father.

Oh, god. Had her mother been trying to leave?

Gia rushed to the bathroom, unsteady on her feet as her head throbbed with renewed vengeance. She made it, pulled back her hair, and lost the meager contents of her stomach into the toilet.

When she'd heaved herself dry, she slumped against the wall, the cold tiles giving her chills through her thin sleep shorts. She shouldn't believe the random caller. There was no reason to think Franco wasn't her biological father or that her mother had cheated. Letti Balzano hadn't betrayed the family.

Gia didn't want to believe it, but she was cold and clammy, like she'd been hit with a sudden fever, her body telling a disturbingly different story than the one she had been fed all these years.

Another memory surfaced, much clearer than the day at the park.

"I've seen Ma with that man before," Marc had said, tucked *away in a blanket fort with Gia. He'd seemed so big, ten years old to her five.*

"What man?"

"The one who took you."

"He didn't take me," Gia had objected.

"He did." Marc grabbed her arm and squeezed. *"You didn't want to go with him. Father said he took you."*

"Okay," Gia agreed, trying to pull her arm free.

Marc didn't let go. "Did you see Ma with him before?"

"Yeah."

Marc's hold tightened, and he looked scared. "Don't tell Father. He'll be angry."

"Okay." Gia's eyes watered. She wanted to leave the blanket fort. Everyone had been so angry lately, but Marc wasn't usually like this.

"Good," he agreed, releasing her. "Sorry. Let's play."

Gia wasn't sure how accurate the memory was. She certainly didn't remember the man now, let alone her mother meeting with him. But the conversation with Marc was long enough ago that it was before her migraines began, so perhaps she could trust it.

Had Marc really seen the kidnapper, the supposed Jeffrey Lockwood, before the kidnapping? With their mother? He'd been aware enough of what that meant to keep it from their father.

Was this the reason no one ever talked about Letti Balzano? Not out of respect for their father's loss, but due to fear of invoking his rage?

Gia closed her eyes. This was ridiculous. She shouldn't let some faceless guy's lies get under her skin. She was probably twisting her memories to fit the seed of doubt the call had planted. It wasn't as if she *wanted* to be related to Franco Balzano. She was seeing what a deep, hidden part of her wanted to see.

Wasn't she?

Gia grabbed her phone and played the voicemail.

"Hello, Gianna. This is your Aunt Susan's lawyer again. Before you delete this, please listen. Your aunt has left her entire estate to you, including documentation regarding your parentage. You need to know the truth. Call me."

TWO

GIA

GIA WAS STILL SITTING on the bathroom floor an hour later when Marc came into her room.

"G?" he called.

"In here."

Marc's head poked through the doorway, his hair and beard trimmed short, every line as sharp as the cut of his suit. "What are you doing on the floor?"

Having an existential crisis. "I can't be fucked today."

Marc snorted. "Get up. I've got your food." He held out a hand, his family crest ring glittering in the bright bathroom lights.

Gia grabbed his hand and pulled herself up.

"You're freezing. How long were you sitting here?" Marc stared at her, his usually concerned expression more assessing than usual. Or was it Gia's imagination?

She pulled away and ducked around him to grab a hoodie off the clothes pile on her armchair. The smell of tomatoes and garlic filled the room, and sure enough, a brown paper bag sat on her dressing table. Gia grabbed it and took the food to her bed.

Marc's focus didn't leave her. "If you need help getting up, you can always call Salvator."

Gia's spine stiffened. "I can get off the floor by myself. I just didn't feel like it."

She bit back the part about not wanting to call Salvator. Marc and her father both liked to pretend Salvator wasn't her minder. A fucking babysitter, like she was still a damn child. He was her *driver*. An *assistant*. An *errands man*.

Whatever you wanted to call Salvator, he was always there. And sure, Gia needed help more often than the rest of the family when her migraines came out of nowhere and took her out of commission alarmingly fast, but Salvator's presence often felt more like that of a guard than an aid. And not a bodyguard, which was another job everyone claimed Salvator filled. No. He was her prison guard. Keeping track of where she went and with whom.

Not that Gia went anywhere these days.

Would her father have let up on the constant surveillance if Gia's condition hadn't worsened the older she'd gotten? It had been terrible when the headaches had first hit around her tenth birthday, but her teen years hadn't been as bad.

Her twenties had been a shitshow so far.

Gia unearthed a warm container from the bag and opened it. Penne alla vodka. Her favorite. Out of everyone in the family, Marc was by far the kindest.

"Thanks for this." Gia grabbed the accompanying fork and dove in. "What are you up to tonight?"

He shoved his hands in his pockets. "I've got to do the rounds. Then I'm meeting the boys. Father's got shit to do too."

So the house would be—well, not empty, it never was—free of her immediate family at least.

"I was thinking about Ma earlier," Gia said smoothly, loading her fork with pasta.

Marc's shoulders stiffened. "Gia..." he said, as if she'd brought up something they'd agreed not to discuss.

"What? We never talk about her."

"What's there to say? She's been dead for twenty years. Come on. Don't do this now. Things are tense. Shit's going down, and Father has enough on his plate as we get ready for the expansion."

"I'm not mentioning her to Father, *Marco*."

His posture relaxed slightly. "Good. And don't say my name like that." He was Marc to all his close friends, as if it was some big honor to drop the O.

"Why can't you and I talk about Ma?" Gia put her fork down. "She died to save me. Why isn't she ever honored? Father goes on about Jake's sacrifice for the family all the damn time, and then he acts like his wife did something wrong."

How had she never seen it so plainly before? Had she really let pain and guilt overshadow everything else? Letti should have been a legend for dying to save one of Franco's children.

Marc's posture sagged, and his expression turned almost pitying. "Drop it, Gia."

"No."

A flash of something like hurt contorted her brother's face. He ran a hand through his hair. "What happened is in the past. Look, I've got to go." He turned toward the door.

Gia's heart jumped into her throat. "What really happened?"

Marc froze. He shot a look over his shoulder, his eyes narrowed. "If that's the question you're asking, then it should be obvious why I don't want to talk about it."

He stormed out of the room, shutting the door behind him.

Gia pushed her food away, feeling sick again. He should have said: *You already know what happened.*

Fuck.

Dying to save her from kidnapping wasn't Letti's whole story, or not the real story. And Marc knew it was a lie. Maybe the memory of them in the blanket fort wasn't total bullshit.

Could the lawyer on the phone have been telling the truth?

Gia's throat constricted. If Franco wasn't her biological father and he'd found out... Had the whole kidnapping thing been a lie to explain away the confusing things she half remembered? To cover up the truth? To shut her up? To save face?

And Marc *knew*.

Gia had to talk to the lawyer, but not on her cellphone. If this turned out to be true, she couldn't risk anyone seeing the calls on the phone records—beyond what was already there—or risk anyone listening in. Her phone probably wasn't tapped because she never did anything interesting as far as her family was concerned, but she couldn't risk it.

Not with something like this.

Most people might struggle to believe their father had their mother killed for having another man's baby, but Gia wasn't most people. Franco absolutely would have. Out of the whole scenario, this was one aspect she didn't doubt. Gia held no illusions about what her father was capable of.

To Franco, women were expendable, there to fill a role. Except for Gia, who was an obligation and only of any use to Franco if she reflected well on him, which was why her illness remained secret. Why Salvator's other job was to make sure nothing exposing happened while Gia was out of the house.

It was easy to believe Franco's attitude toward Letti had been similar, and if she'd had an affair, borne someone else's child, and that man had come to take Gia away and expose it all, Franco wouldn't have hesitated to eliminate the threat to his image.

∼

Several hours later, Gia brought her food to the kitchen to throw away. "Hi, Mary." She smiled at one of the housekeepers. "Seems quiet around here."

The older woman nodded seriously. "Everyone cleared out. The girls and I won't know what to do without the usual interruptions. Shall I heat dinner for you?"

"No, that's okay, thanks. Marc brought me food."

Mary pretended she hadn't seen Gia throw the food away. "Very good. Let me know if you change your mind." She slipped out of the room.

Gia headed to the library. It seemed lying around all day had been enough to rid her of the worst of last night's effects. She wasn't even tired as she selected a few books and returned to the hall, looking up and down to make sure the coast was clear.

She passed the gym and opened the door to the garage. The one with the SUVs, not the sports cars. But a ride wasn't the reason Gia was here.

Glancing over her shoulder one more time and seeing no one, she hurried to a storage bench at the side of the room. After opening a few drawers, she found what she needed and grabbed it.

Her heart raced, and she quickly selected a set of keys from the line of hooks to unlock the SUV Salvator always drove her around in. She opened the back door, found the bag she'd left behind yesterday, and stowed her items inside.

"Gia?" a deep voice called.

Her heart skipped, but she didn't flinch. She could thank her father for her poker face. Masking emotion was a necessary survival skill growing up around here.

"Hi, Salvator." Gia closed the car door and feigned a tired smile in his direction.

He loomed in the doorway, arms crossed over his singlet,

gold chains gleaming. Combined with dyed jet-black hair, gelled to within an inch of its life, he was a walking stereotype.

Salvator scanned the garage. "What are you doing?"

"Forgot my bag." Gia raised it in the air for his inspection.

He grunted, and his assessing gaze relaxed. "You should be resting."

Gia grabbed the books she'd placed on the roof of the car. "I know, but I needed something to read. Then I remembered my bag. I'm heading upstairs now."

"Good."

Gia kept her face blank as she crossed the room, her movements slow but not so exaggerated that they'd make Salvator suspicious.

When she reached the doorway, Salvator took the key from her and stepped out of the way, allowing her to pass. He didn't follow, and once she escaped his scrutiny, some of her tension eased, but she didn't dare to pick up her pace.

In her bedroom, Gia turned on some music and locked herself in the bathroom. She pulled the burner phone and new prepaid SIM card out of her bag and tore open the plastic casings.

How many times had she seen her father's men grab phones from that drawer? She never thought she'd need one.

Maybe she should have known better.

Once the phone was set up and plugged in to charge, Gia ran the bath. She didn't really think Salvator or anyone was outside her bedroom door listening, but everything about today made her paranoid.

With the water running, she called the number the lawyer had left in his voicemail.

"Hello, Edward Ramirez speaking," said a familiar voice.

"It's Gianna." She glared at herself in the mirror. Fuck, she looked like she'd pulled an all-nighter partying, not passed out with a debilitating headache.

"Gianna, thank you for returning my call. Is this a better number to reach you on?"

She chewed her lip. "Sure. What documentation do you have?"

"Regarding your father, Jeffrey?" He paused, but she didn't respond. "I have photos of him and your mother. A photo of all three of you. Letters from your mother, sent to Jeffrey. Things of that nature."

Of course, her birth certificate would list Franco as her father. "Photos can be faked."

"True. I have the negatives as well."

Right. The photos would be on film black then. Could negatives be faked? Surely not as easily as something digital. "Is that all?" Gia asked.

"No. Your aunt kept everything she had relating to her brother and you, but it's all unofficial. A...um...DNA test would provide the most conclusive proof."

Goddammit. This was actually happening. Gia sank to the floor. "I can't do a DNA test. And you can't send me any of those photos. Nothing about this can arrive at my house," she said, in case the lawyer had found her address along with her number.

"I can text a picture through if you're doubtful. Otherwise, I don't know how to show you, except in person."

And lead Salvator straight to this guy? Not a chance. "Meeting would be a terrible idea for you. I can't get anywhere without..." Wait. Why was she telling him anything?

Ramirez proved unfazed by her implications, continuing on as normal. "Your aunt made me aware of the problem your family poses. She tried to contact you over the years."

"Well, she failed." Gia would obsess about Susan later.

"She may have failed to get ahold of you in her life, but she made it her dying wish to bring you home. All you need to do is finalize everything with me, and there's a condo waiting. A business."

What? This guy had a whole new life waiting for her?

She imagined leaving her family behind and staring over. God, she wanted nothing more than to escape. To clean her conscience of the crimes they committed, all the bad they brought to the world that she did nothing about.

Maybe she could even do something to stop them if she were free.

Gia's stomach twisted, and she banged a fist against the counter. Stop the Balzano family? How? Rival gangs couldn't even get the drop on her father. Who was she? No one but the weak daughter. She couldn't even run away.

What would she do when she got sick on her own? What if she were in public when a migraine stole her consciousness? How could she take over her aunt's business when she routinely couldn't get out of bed?

Helplessness threatened to swallow Gia whole.

She pushed it away. "Do you know what happened to my mother?" she asked the lawyer.

He let out a sad little sound. "I don't know exactly how she died, but she and Jeffrey were planning to take you away from Ashton Lakes to move in with Susan. This is all according to Susan herself. I never knew Jeffrey. Susan said Letti and Jeffrey never made it to Shearwater Landing, and when Susan looked into it, she found Letti's obituary. Officially, Jeffrey is still missing, but well, it's been twenty years."

A wave of darkness washed over Gia, and she thought it might obliterate her.

"Text me the picture of them together. I'll call you back."

Gia hung up and clapped a hand over her mouth, stifling a choking sob, her chest hollowing out.

She didn't doubt the lawyer anymore. Why would he make this up? Her father was the one with a motive to lie, and the means—not to mention mentality—to pull off a double murder and cover it up.

Franco had killed her mother, hadn't he? And then he'd looked Gia in the face every day since and lied about *everything*.

Fuck this. Fuck staying here and tiptoeing around the man who'd killed someone he was supposed to love. It wasn't as if Gia had never thought of running away before. She had, but she'd always been too scared.

Well, screw that.

Screw everyone who said she couldn't survive on her own. She knew she wasn't weak, even if her father never missed a chance to tell her otherwise. Even if she'd let his judgments seep under her skin, keeping her trapped and dependent.

This was her life, and she was going to start living it on her terms.

THREE
AURORA

Aurora Thornfield clenched her fists on her lap in an effort not to scream. She stared down the long table at her mother, who sat silently beside her uncle as he spelled out Aurora's fate.

"This alliance is vital for the coven, and Arthur Nightingale has been most accommodating. His son will be here in two weeks for a betrothal feast. The wedding—I think the Nightingales will agree—should be held shortly after. At the new moon."

Aurora pounced on the pause in his monologue. "Wouldn't binding oaths between leaders be a more secure way to begin an alliance than marriage? Why leave room for—"

"Silence until I've finished speaking, child. I didn't ask for your input." Stan Thornfield, leader of their coven, glared at her as if she were no more than a nuisance.

Aurora didn't bother protesting being called a child at age twenty-five. It wasn't a hill worth dying on. The rest, however... "It's my life. I get a say in who I *marry*."

"*Aurora*." Her mother, Virginia Thornfield, was red-faced, her glare even fiercer than Stan's.

Aurora's uncle raised his hand. Magic flared, and Aurora's heart sank. A silencing spell wound around her throat like ice, yet her blood boiled.

Uncle Stan smirked. "It is your duty to support the coven, Aurora. As any lady should. Harper Nightingale will be the kind of husband you need if he's anything like his father. The Nightingales are exemplary. Their coven is powerful, and you're well aware that allying with like-minded worshipers of our Damned Lord is more important now than ever. Especially with covens from outside our region."

Because sane covens didn't tolerate Satan worshipers like the Thornfields. Not when their bullshit leaked out of their compounds and into the community.

Uncle Stan barreled on. "Since you've expressed no interest in dating anyone *suitable*, not a single man or woman committed to Satan, you're perfectly placed to make this match. As close to a daughter of my own as I have."

Murmurs of agreement sounded around the table. The room was full of men—all Stan's trusted advisors and enforcers. A group of arrogant people who thought they could tell Aurora who to marry, and the thought made her sick.

No, it made her murderous.

Each and every one of these sorry excuses for witches was lucky that the forced blood loyalty running through her veins prevented her from striking against them, or they'd all burn.

Blood loyalty was old, evil magic. Aurora couldn't attack or cast spells against any member of the Thornfield Coven who outranked her, and of course, they all did. Obedience had been sewn into her skin. From birth, the magic running through her betrayed her by enforcing a hierarchy controlled by the coven leader. Everyone at the top was untouchable, and those who weren't were at their mercy.

That much control would have been bad enough, but her

coven had taken blood binding a step further. Preventing vulnerable members from fighting back was all well and good until those people ran away. To close this last remaining door, Stan had bound their bloodline to the very land they lived on.

Aurora was tied to the coven's compound by her magic, by her very blood and bones, held in place by the dirt beneath her feet, though she wasn't permanently confined. Everyone in the coven moved about wider society to some extent, but Stan had the power to recall Aurora to coven land and stop her from leaving.

As long as she was tied to this place, Aurora would never be free. But she'd been working on a way around the binding. Seemed she needed to speed up her escape timeline. Immediately.

Aurora's mother began talking about the engagement feast, acting as if trading her daughter for access to another coven's power was some kind of honor. To Virginia, it probably was. She was as bad as Uncle Stan, seeing as she'd happily step on everyone around her to push herself up.

"Once married, the couple will remain here. At least for the immediate future," Uncle Stan said to his advisors. "The Nightingales have important business in the city, and I've offered our help."

Aurora shuddered to think what business it could be. Not that her uncle would tell her. Would her new brute of a husband keep it from her, too? Probably.

Aurora's skin crawled, her heart racing as she faced a future under yet another person's control. The walls closed in. Aurora had been trapped her whole life, but suddenly, the feeling was unbearable, dark, and consuming. It strangled her chest until her thoughts scattered, leaving behind an aching hollowness.

She had a way through this. The only way to survive. Urgency to act now, to run from the room, clawed at her insides, but she stayed still as her relatives' useless words washed over her.

At last, the meeting ended, and Aurora was dismissed. The silencing spell unwound from her throat, and she stormed out of the room.

"Stay close," Uncle Stan called after her as if it were a request, rather than an order she had no power to disobey. "Your new husband wouldn't like you out around the city with Satan knows who."

Aurora's back stiffened, her footsteps faltering ever so slightly before continuing along the hall. She grabbed her jacket and slid it over her mesh top and bralette combo. She'd been planning to go out anyway, and was surprised her outfit hadn't garnered a comment or two from her uncle or mother.

They really must have been focused on the marriage arrangement and alliance to pass up the opportunity to criticize her.

Her hands delved into the jacket pockets and found them empty. Patting them frantically, Aurora cursed under her breath.

"Looking for this?" Her mother had followed. She held Aurora's phone with a smug look on her slender face.

"Why do you have my phone?"

"You heard your uncle. No more gallivanting around. You have more important things to focus on, like the rituals to prepare you for marriage."

Aurora stared at the woman, her magic sparking uselessly inside her. "I'm not marrying anyone."

"Suck it up, Aurora. This is part of life. We all have to make sacrifices. The coven is more important than what you want."

Aurora wanted to scream. "I'm going for a walk."

"Fine. You can't go far. Stan won't allow you off the grounds until this deal is done." Virginia pointedly slid Aurora's phone into her pocket. "The moonlight will be good for you. Try to be in a better mood when you return. It'll make things easier."

For her, maybe, but Aurora wasn't playing along. Her mother and Uncle Stan would have to invoke all the power of the blood binding to get her anywhere near this scummy Nightingale witch.

Aurora slammed the front door on her way out and stalked into the woods. As she passed the main altar, she pocketed four candles. There was no time to search for a safer spell. She'd *never* walk into that house again. Never be a servant to a man who came from a coven like hers. Someone as entitled and cruel as her uncle.

She wouldn't. No matter what it took.

Aurora went as deep into the woods as she could without leaving Thornfield land. The binding tugged on her skin, itching like a rash and reminding her she wasn't allowed to leave.

Not all covens were like this. Aurora had friends in the city who belonged to a coven that valued respect, autonomy, common decency, and had no use for amassing power.

Virginia might have prevented her from sending an SOS by taking her phone, but it wasn't the end of the world. Her friends couldn't help with the first part of her plan anyway.

Being an hour outside Shearwater Landing wasn't the insurmountable issue. It wasn't as if Aurora could simply call for a ride and be free. She had to break the blood binding. Once she accomplished that, she'd walk out of the woods, through the suburbs, and into the city, no matter how long it took. She'd quite literally walk over hot coals or to the ends of the Earth if she had to.

She could do anything once she was free.

Aurora set the candles in the dirt, marking north, south, east, and west. With a flick of her wrist, the wicks ignited.

A spell like this was impossible to practice. There were no trial runs, but any hesitation weighing Aurora down had fled.

It was time to put her theory to the test.

Aurora shrugged off her jacket and lay at the center of the candles, the traitorous earth cool through her clothes even on a warm summer night. She dug her fingernails into the topsoil and ran her plan through one last time.

To break the ties binding her, Aurora needed to separate herself from everything holding her back. Her essence—her soul, her most essential self—couldn't be constrained in its purest form. That was a fact.

Along with the gift of magic, witches had an understanding of the universe that humans simply didn't. The Human Realm wasn't the sole plane of existence. Witches had been created by Lucifer, a fallen Eternal being who had fled the afterlife to live on Earth. The history of the Devil, demons, and witches revealed that, after death, all mortal souls entered one afterlife or another. Humans reincarnated and thus went to the Eternal Realm, and witches went to the Realm of the Damned.

In the end, they all became souls, and *nothing* on Earth could influence or contain such a pure form of existence.

Aurora had researched the magic of soul theory extensively. She wasn't the first witch to experiment with life, mortality, and what lay beyond. Based on the work of those who came before her, she'd constructed a spell to free herself. Her work was solid, the magic grounded in undisputed facts.

But it was risky.

Her friends in the Lockwood Coven had begged her to find another way. They promised to break her free themselves. But they couldn't. It wasn't that easy, even if Aurora hadn't run out of time to stage a rescue. The Thornfields weren't weak, and the Lockwoods weren't powermongers or fighters. It was part of what made them good. All Aurora needed from the Lockwoods was a safe place to land once she saved herself.

Her theory was airtight, she reminded herself one last time, pretending her heart wasn't pounding and her dirt-covered palms weren't sweating. Her soul existed regardless of her mortal vessel. When she died, she'd pass on to the same afterlife all witches were destined to.

But dying wasn't what Aurora wanted, even knowing death wasn't the end. She couldn't go on like this, but life was precious. Her years on Earth couldn't all be spent in a cage. She had to escape. She *would*. Then everything would be better. The potential for change meant there was always hope.

She could do this.

Aurora would free herself by leaving her body. Freeing her soul of all earthly ties. But she couldn't die, or she'd leave this realm never to return. She had to fake it. Hover in between. Separate her soul from her flesh while she still lived, leaving her body suspended in life.

Then, once she broke free from her mortal chains, she could reenter her body and be free. Her magic—rooted in her soul—would be her own.

Yes, magic ran through the blood in her veins, but it went where her soul went. A dead witch held no power, their blood no different than a human's once life fled, and while Aurora wasn't dying, the fact remained: magic followed the soul. So, Aurora would separate her magic and her blood, break her power free, and then return to an unbound body.

She dug her fingers deeper into the dirt. Her heart beat rapidly, her head light and vision blurring, but she wouldn't let nerves sway her. *This will work.* It was worth it. She wasn't afraid to face death and cheat it.

Aurora cleared her aching throat, ignored her wet, stinging eyes, and recited the spell she'd so carefully constructed.

Her magic sparked, and tingles shot through her body as if the very blood in her veins was vibrating. She gripped the earth, forcing her eyes to remain open as she continued the spell. The candle flames flared. Heat rose, and sweat gathered at her brow.

Aurora's words didn't falter, and as the last syllable passed her lips, something deep within her jolted, pain radiating from her chest. She gasped a rattling breath and lurched forward, head spinning, her vision darkening until she saw nothing but black.

Her vision cleared in an instant. She was floating, looking down at herself, blonde hair splayed out in the dirt, eyes closed, chest unmoving. But her cheeks remained rosy with life.

She'd done it!

Elation filled Aurora, fizzing like a thousand tiny bubbles.

Abruptly, the candles around her body snuffed out, and something tugged at the back of her brain. No, not her brain, her consciousness? Before Aurora could react, the force swept her soul away.

Leaving her body behind.

FOUR

GIA

"Gia, it's good to see you at the table," Franco said as he joined her and Marc for dinner.

It had been three days, and Gia had avoided her family even more than usual. She smiled sweetly. "Good to see you too, Father. You've been so busy."

A smug expression tugged at Franco's lips. He'd aged unfairly well and always dressed impeccably. Marc had picked up Franco's meticulous grooming habits, but their resemblance went beyond fashion sense, leaving no doubt they were related by blood.

Gia had always assumed the differences between her and her father and brother were due to taking after her mother. Her features were finer, her hair darker, but her tanned complexion and brown eyes fit in well enough with the rest of the family.

The truth lay in the details she'd overlooked. Seeing the picture of Jeffrey Lockwood that Ramirez had sent, it was clear she had his nose. Not her mother's or Franco's.

Franco waved a heavily ringed hand, and one of the men standing silently at the edge of the room disappeared into the kitchen. "You know me, Gianna. There's always someone testing my patience. Never mind plenty of work to do. If I bothered to rest, all this would be taken away." He gestured around the opulent dining room.

He never missed a chance to imply rest was weak. Renewed anger surged through Gia, but she withheld her retort.

Mary entered with dinner and deftly transferred the various dishes from her cart to the table as the lackey returned to his silent place by the door.

"Nothing will be taken away. We'll figure out who's moving against us soon enough," Marc said, reaching for one of the dishes.

Franco hummed. "As long as dealing with the problem doesn't cut into our plans. Looking beyond Ashton Lakes is well overdue."

"Of course," Marc agreed.

Gia didn't want to hear it. Listening to Franco express his never-ending need for more was exhausting. She served herself and let the others settle into eating for a few minutes before turning to her brother. "Are you stopping by Poison tonight?" It was the Balzanos' most popular nightclub.

Marc's brows rose. "Yeah. I have to check on a few things. Why?"

Gia shrugged. "I'm dying to go dancing. Do something. You know?"

"Really?" Marc's gaze darted to their father to check his reaction.

"*Gianna.*" Franco tutted right on cue. "Is that really a good idea?"

She forced herself to stay calm, her voice taking on a whiny, rather than desperate, edge. "Why not? I've been feeling great for days. All I've done is rest. Please. I need to get out of the house for a bit."

Franco's eyes narrowed. "You're not meeting someone, are you?"

God forbid she have a friend or a date. "It's not like that, I promise. I'll be with Marc and Salvator."

Marc caught her eye and flashed her a smile. "It's best if Gia goes to one of our clubs. Come on, she needs a little fun. The boys and I will look out for her."

Gia's pulse spiked, and her father's gaze narrowed in her direction, almost as if he could tell. Marc meant well, but his comment was infuriating. Was it too much to ask to be treated like an adult and not someone who needed supervision?

Fuck, she had to get out of here. How had she done this for so long?

Franco dabbed at his mouth with a napkin. "You're right, Marc. But you'll be fully responsible."

"Nothing will happen, Father," he promised.

Gia hated him for accepting the way Franco treated her. Whatever. She'd take it as a sign she needn't feel guilty about the punishment Marc would inevitably receive for her actions tonight.

The picture the lawyer had sent her was burned into Gia's mind. Her mother and Jeffrey, with a toddler between them. With *Gia* between them. They'd looked happy, but she couldn't imagine how Ma had thought things could work out when she'd been married to Franco Balzano.

Gia felt trapped and watched. Had it been the same for her mother?

"Shall we leave at ten-thirty?" Gia asked her brother as if the insulting exchange hadn't happened.

Marc pulled out his phone. "Make it ten. I'll ride with you and Salvator, and text Jay to bring his girlfriend, so you won't be bored while I talk shop. You know Tessa and the girls. I'm sure they'll all come along."

Yes, Gia knew Tessa and her friends, all of whom moved in organized crime circles. Gia hadn't socialized with any of them since high school, though she'd run into them at various events over the years.

Gia glanced at her father, knowing he expected her to check for approval.

He nodded, his face impassive and eyes cold. "Home by two."

"Yes, Father."

GIA GRABBED Salvator's to-go cup of coffee from Mary on her way out of the house. She stopped in the bathroom by the gym and quickly added a laxative. A moment later, she was sauntering into the garage, designer bag slung over her shoulder, and a smile on her face.

"I've got you coffee, Salvator." She handed him the cup.

"Grazie." He had a sip, looking distinctly grumpy to be leaving the house this late at night. At least he was too well-trained to complain about her impromptu excursion.

Gia settled in the back seat and pulled out her phone, pretending to look busy. Her pulse pounded. If she got caught tonight, she might never be allowed out of the house again, but her reclusive lifestyle and willingness to follow her family's rules without a fight meant no one would suspect she was up to anything.

Marc slid into the seat beside her and bumped her shoulder. "Damn. I didn't know you owned dresses like that."

Gia generally favored button-up shirts and sweaters. Tonight's outfit was skin tight except for the short, frilly skirt, which puffed out around her hips. Cute and very impractical. "You look the same as always, Marc."

He snorted. "Let's go, Salvator."

The man was already reversing out of the garage. "Yes, boss."

Marc's phone rang, and he answered it with a grumble, shooting an apologetic look in Gia's direction. What a relief. She hadn't been looking forward to chatting. The less she said, the less likely Marc was to pick up on her nerves.

Would this plan work?

Franco would be enraged the second he realized she was gone. She had to make sure she wasn't found, and wouldn't have known how to accomplish that without Susan's lawyer.

She'd verified some of Ramirez's story through public records. Her aunt's death. Her relation to Jeffrey and the existence of the theater Susan had owned. Gia didn't doubt what he'd told her, but she was trusting his offer to help her flee without having a clue why he'd want to assist. Escaping a crime family wasn't usual lawyer business.

But trusting Ramirez was Gia's only option. She had no one else, and she couldn't wait long enough to come up with another plan. The longer she stayed, the higher the chance she'd slip up, and Franco would discover what she knew.

Then she'd never get out.

Twenty minutes later, Salvator pulled up at the club. "Shall I wait out here or follow you in, boss?"

Marc ended his call. "Wait here. I'll call if I need you."

"Sure thing." Salvator had another sip of coffee and got out to open Gia's door.

She suppressed a smirk and adjusted her dress. Salvator would no doubt be occupied by the time Marc called to say there was a problem.

Marc appeared at her side and laughed. "Could you have brought a bigger bag, G?"

She rolled her eyes, her hold tightening on the massive

purse. "It's designer. You're the one who invited Tessa. She'll love it. It's called a conversation starter, genius."

"Sure. Great. Come on." Marc had already lost interest and ushered her toward the entrance.

"Evening, Marco," the doorman said, his eyes lingering on Gia. "Shit going down tonight?"

"What?" Marc snapped, stopping to glare. "No, we're good. Chill."

The man's expression turned stricken. "Apologies, Marco. Everyone is already at your table."

The annoyance faded from Marc's face, and he clapped the guy on the shoulder. "Good man."

Gia followed him into the club, noise hitting her like a slap to the face. *Ugh*, she was not a club girl. Lights and loud noises overwhelmed her even when they didn't necessarily trigger her migraines.

Marc led Gia to a roped-off area where his friends sat with a bunch of women, some of whom Gia recognized, and many more she didn't. Marc shouted introductions to a few people and snapped at his friends to behave themselves.

Gia barely heard any of it, and not because of the music. She was buzzing out of her skin, counting the seconds until she could slip away.

Tessa disentangled from her boyfriend and came over. "Gia, babe. It's been for-fucking-ever. Love your dress."

"Thanks." Gia's cheeks heated. Tessa was beautiful, and despite what Gia had said to Marc, didn't give a shit about designer bags. At least not any more than your typical rich person did. "How've you been?"

Tessa tossed her silken hair over her shoulder, exposing her collarbone and slender neck. "Ugh, bored. We should dance."

Gia's stomach flipped. "Totally. Let me put this in Marc's office." She gestured to the damn bag.

Tessa chuckled, but more like she thought Gia's inappropriate accessory was cute than like she was making fun. "Hurry back. Okay?"

Gia nodded, and Tessa turned to one of the other women, placing a hand on her elbow as she leaned in to speak to her.

Gia swallowed, her throat parched. Tessa had always been like that, touchy and incredibly friendly. Gia had spent a great deal of time in high school hoping it had meant something more. It hadn't.

She elbowed her brother. "I'm going to leave this in your office."

Marc shook his head like he found her ridiculous. "Knew your bag was too much. Let's go. I've got to check a few things upstairs anyway."

Gia gritted her teeth, but she'd suspected he wouldn't leave her side so soon. Protesting his presence would only backfire. She'd have to wait for Marc to get bored of following her around.

They navigated the crowd to the rear stairs, where two men stood guard, preventing patrons from wandering into the office area.

"Marco, can I have a word?" one of the men asked as they approached.

Marc crossed his arms, inclining his chin. "Sure, what's up?"

Gia seized her chance. "I'll run to your office while you guys talk."

Marc grabbed her shoulder, halting her. "Who's up there?" he asked the guard.

"Top floor's empty at the moment. Todd's in the control room behind the bar. He's got some footage you should see. Sooner rather than later."

Marc sighed. "Shit. Go on, Gia." He pointed a menacing,

ringed finger at the guards. "She stays upstairs alone or waits here with you until I return. No one else goes up. Got it?"

They nodded so seriously you'd think Marc had asked them to look after live explosives. Gia could have rolled her eyes. The sheer drama.

Marc headed down the hall toward the security room and was soon out of sight. Gia hurried up the stairs. The top floor was deserted, as promised, and she slipped into Marc's office, shutting the door behind her.

There were no cameras in here. It was one of the few places in the club that wasn't under surveillance. Gia set her purse on Marc's desk and pulled out the backpack she'd hidden within, leaving her wallet and regular phone behind.

Sweat beaded at the nape of her neck. Holy fuck, this was happening.

She took the backpack into the adjoining bathroom and pulled out the hoodie and leggings she'd packed along with the ten grand in cash she'd had stashed in her room. Gia might not have accomplished much over the years, but she wasn't naïve. She'd been tucking money away forever.

She pulled the clothes on, not wasting time removing her tight dress. The skirt tucked into the hoodie well enough and was out of the way. She swapped her heels for flats and powered on her burner phone.

Unknown: All set.

Her ride was waiting. Gia replied with a thumbs up and climbed out the bathroom window and down the fire escape. She didn't look back.

A CAR with the license plate Ramirez had sent through sat around the corner from the rear of the club. Gia opened the back door and slid in. The door had barely shut before the car was pulling into traffic.

"Hey, I'm Sam, a friend of your aunt's," said the woman in the driver's seat, catching Gia's eye in the rearview mirror.

Gia was lost for what to say. Her heart pounded so fast, she feared she'd pass out. Fuck, if she got one of her headaches now, she'd cry. The car's heavy herbal scent wasn't helping.

Sam didn't seem bothered by her lack of response. "Can you let Ramirez know we're on our way?"

Gia nodded and sent the text. She craned her neck to get a look at the street behind them, but didn't see anyone giving chase. Not a single black SUV in sight.

That was too easy. Surely someone had seen her on the back alley camera. Even with a change of clothes, she wasn't impossible to recognize, and they'd investigate anyone poking around regardless of whether they realized it was her. Unless Marc and the security guys were too busy with whatever footage had them concerned.

Gia's tense muscles loosened as Sam pulled onto the highway. The woman was silent, her focus on the road, and Gia found herself relaxing into the calm. No one was following. She was safe for now.

$\sim$

GIA JOLTED awake and rubbed her dry eyes. Where was she? Her head pounded. Fuck, she was in a car.

That's right, she'd escaped.

Sam was driving down a deserted stretch of highway. The clock on the dash said it was past three in the morning. Gia couldn't believe she'd slept for hours, but it didn't feel like she'd had one of her migraines, so she hadn't lost time. At least not yet.

She glanced over her shoulder and out the rear window, finding no cars in sight. Good.

Digging through her backpack, she pulled out one of her pill bottles. She'd packed every bottle she'd had on hand before leaving. Once she was settled in Shearwater Landing, she'd have to find a doctor to prescribe more, but she'd be fine for months.

"There's water in the center console."

Gia jolted at the sound of Sam's voice, looking over to find the woman's heavily lined eyes on her in the rear-view mirror.

"Thanks." She grabbed a sealed bottle and took her pill. "Headache," she explained, not wanting Sam to wonder. Gia hadn't mentioned her condition to Ramirez. It wasn't anyone's business.

Sam nodded, refocused on the road. "I need to stop for gas soon. Grab some food and anything else you need while I fill up."

"Will do." Gia checked her burner phone and brought up a

map. They'd made it out of state, but the West Coast was still nearly thirty hours away without stopping.

"Are we staying somewhere for the night?" she asked.

"Technically, it's morning. And no. We'll get back on the road after we refuel, so use the restroom."

Unease twisted Gia's gut. Sam didn't appear tired, and Gia couldn't deny putting as much distance as possible between her and Ashton Lakes was the safest bet.

It was fine. They'd have to stop eventually.

THEY DID NOT STOP EVENTUALLY, and Gia was beginning to wonder if Sam was human. Which was bonkers. The kind of thing you'd only consider while sleep deprived and hopped up on too much caffeine.

Of course the woman was human. But Sam hadn't slept at all, and she seemed as fresh as a fucking daisy.

Gia felt like she'd been hit by a bus. It had been nearly two days of only drive-throughs and quick stops at gas stations. The breakneck pace was a solid strategy to lose any pursuers. But still.

Who the fuck *was* Sam? Was it normal for lawyers to have associates who picked up random people in the middle of the night and drove halfway across the country like a bat out of Hell? No, it wasn't.

And these people were friends with my aunt?

What if Gia had escaped one gang for another? It would be just her luck. Why hadn't she considered that? True, she'd been distracted by the whole Franco-isn't-your-biological-father thing, *but still.* She should have asked more questions before trapping herself in a car with a woman who didn't need to sleep.

"You good?" Sam asked, almost as if she could sense Gia panicking.

"Fine, but I need to get out of this car. How are you not fried after driving for so long?"

"I don't need much sleep," Sam said as if her driving-without-stopping superpower was nothing special.

Gia couldn't bring herself to ask for clarification. She'd get to Shearwater Landing, claim her inheritance, and then never see Ramirez or Sam again. And if these people and her aunt had been into some dodgy shit? Well, Gia would have some choices to make, but she was not letting anyone control her life. Never again.

An hour later, Sam exited the highway. The sun rose over Shearwater Landing, glinting off an impressive skyline. This city was much larger than Ashton Lakes. See, Franco didn't control the entire world. Gia tried to take comfort in the reminder.

Sam navigated the city streets with ease, passing through the tallest buildings and leaving them behind. Eventually, she pulled over on a rundown block of closed shops.

Sam pulled the parking brake and twisted around. "I called Edward while you were sleeping. He's upstairs waiting for you. Would you like me to give you a ride to Susan's place, uh, your new place, after you sign the papers?"

"You don't have to," Gia said automatically.

"Obligation isn't why I offered." Sam smiled, and Gia realized it was the first time she'd seen the woman do so. She didn't look much older than Gia despite the mature impression her calm authority gave.

"No, it's all right. You must be dying to get home and sleep." Gia paused as a thought occurred. "Are you from Ashton Lakes?"

"Never been there before in my life."

"Oh..." Gia's pulse quickened for reasons she couldn't put her finger on. "Do you live here?"

"Not in the Banks, no. That's the neighborhood we're in," Sam added in response to Gia's blank look. "I'm in the Arts District, but I'm sure I'll see you around once you settle in."

"Maybe." Gia had no clue why Sam assumed they'd reconnect. This wasn't a small town where you ran into people all the time, and despite the massive favor, they hadn't struck up a friendship. "Thanks for helping me."

Sam's stoic expression turned alarmingly tender. "Of course. We've been trying to find a way to get to you for years."

A chill ran down Gia's spine. What the hell? Yeah, the lawyer mentioned Susan had tried to contact her, but contact was a far cry from *getting to her*. And Susan's attempts had nothing to do with Sam.

Whatever Susan had done over the years, she couldn't have tried very hard. Ramirez had tracked her down and ferried her away easily enough.

This was smelling more and more like organized crime. Or something dodgy.

"I really appreciate your help," Gia repeated as she grabbed her backpack and opened the door. She did appreciate it, but she didn't trust this woman.

SIX
AURORA

For the life of her, Aurora couldn't figure out where she was.

Okay. She was in a room with a desk. She knew that much.

But *why* didn't this room have any windows?

She screamed, the sound deafening to her own ears, even though she had no physical ears. No vocal cords. No body.

Was the sound of her scream all in her mind? No, she didn't have a mind either. No neurons firing. Aurora was a spirit. A ghost. And no one responded to her cries of rage.

Without a body, Aurora couldn't open the door to the room, the desk drawers, or the cabinets lining the wall. If she held her hands in front of her face, she saw a pale outline of her former self, but she had no physical presence. She could feel the desk when she placed her hand against it, the wood preventing her from passing through, but that was all.

Apparently, she existed enough to be confined, but not enough to have any impact on the world around her. And she had no way of knowing if anyone could hear her cries for help.

Despair clawed at her.

She had to retrieve her body. How had she escaped the

Thornfield compound and ended up trapped in this damned room? It made no sense.

Aurora called on her magic but found nothing within. She shook, an icy sensation enveloping her every time she tried.

She should have access to her magic. Why didn't she?

Damnation, she'd fucked this up, even if she wasn't dead. Her body was still alive—suspended by her spell and waiting for her return—otherwise she'd be in the Realm of the Damned. But even if she was still in the Human Realm, she'd been separated from her body for too long. Her lifeless form would have been found, and she didn't know what her family would do with her.

EDWARD RAMIREZ HAD way too many candles for a lawyer. They lined the windowsill. His desk. The many shelves. New candles. Half-melted candles. Little stubby wax ends that most people would have thrown away.

Even more worrying were the odd, unlabeled bottles littering the room. It all added up to a bad omen. Fuck, Gia didn't even believe in omens. She wasn't superstitious. She believed in no higher power. But something about being here sent her mind down a fantastical path.

Was this what sleep deprivation did to a person?

Gia was bound to get a migraine soon, but before she could address self-care, she had to get the hell out of Ramirez's creepy office.

Really, he'd been nothing but kind. Unless he'd been *too* kind? Gia couldn't help second-guessing. Nothing seemed simple after that strange car ride.

Ramirez placed a key on his cluttered desk. "Now all the paperwork is taken care of, here's the key to Susan's condo, and these"—he placed a ring of keys next to the first—"are for the theater."

"I can't thank you enough." Gia slipped the keys into her hoodie pocket. She needed a shower and a change of clothes as badly as she needed to get away from this man and all his candles.

Ramirez gave her a warm smile. "We're happy to help. I know you must be exhausted, but there's more to go over."

"More?" Gia grabbed the stack of manila folders he'd given her. "Wait. What *we* are you talking about?"

He wasn't giving organized crime vibes, but who knew how they did things on the West Coast?

Ramirez leaned back in his chair. "We as in the Lockwoods."

Gia almost laughed in relief. He meant her newfound family. "Are you part of the family?" Maybe he'd married in.

"No. I mean the Lockwood Coven. My membership isn't obvious since I use my legal last name for business, but I'm a Lockwood too."

Gia stood, her chair scraping backward. *Coven?* No. No way.

"It's cool if my Aunt Susan was Wiccan or whatever, but I'm not interested in hearing about your religion."

Ramirez chuckled. "It's not a religion. Not for us anyway. Witches and Wiccans aren't the same. Susan wondered if we'd need to fill you in."

"No, really. I don't need to be. I'm good." Gia took a step toward the door.

She wouldn't lie, she was relieved Susan hadn't been involved with a gang or something criminal in nature, but she did not need this guy to try to recruit her to his cult.

Witches. Did he think he could do spells? No wonder he had so many candles.

Ramirez opened his mouth, but Gia cut him off. "I need to

sleep and get organized. I can hardly think straight right now. If I have any questions, I'll call."

"Okay." He sounded reluctant, but didn't push.

Was he respecting her boundaries? He was one of the few people in her life who bothered, and that was fucking sad.

As novel as basic respect was, Gia still wasn't hearing Ramirez out. She did not survive the emotional turmoil that Catholicism had brought into her life to get sucked into something else, regardless of what Ramirez said about his coven not being religious.

Gia said goodbye and got the hell out of there, her backpack stuffed with papers, cash, pills, and her club dress. *Jesus.*

For a brief moment, Gia wished she hadn't sent Sam and her offer of a ride away, but if Sam was in the same *coven* as Ramirez, it was for the best. Susan's condo, now Gia's, wasn't terribly far away.

Gia walked through the modest neighborhood, following the directions on her burner phone's map, and came to a narrow, tidily kept building across the street from the Spotlight Theater, which she now owned.

She unearthed the residential building's entry code from her pile of papers and let herself inside. The condo was on the third floor with one other unit beside it.

Gia unlocked the door and stepped inside.

Ramirez had mentioned that Susan's things had been cleared out, but the lack of personality in the space was jarring. There was no art on the walls. No décor. The furniture had been left, and a quick walk-through and a peek into the closets revealed no personal effects.

Gia had no complaints. She hadn't been looking forward to living in someone else's home, especially someone she hadn't known.

She found a shopping bag full of clothes in the middle of the living room floor, and a closer inspection revealed the items generally matched her size. How considerate and creepy.

Who'd bought these?

Gia had the urge to toss the bag out the front door, but she couldn't spend another second in these leggings, and she wasn't even wearing a shirt under her hoodie.

After showering and changing her clothes, Gia felt more functional. She swallowed a pill in the hopes the dull ache in her head wouldn't get worse, and stretched out on the couch, too tired to make the bed with the new linens she'd seen in the laundry cupboard.

She shut her eyes.

Knock. Knock.

Gia jolted awake with no idea how long she'd been asleep.

She hauled herself up with effort. At the door, she peered through the peephole. A woman she didn't recognize stood on the other side.

Gia opened the door a crack. "Hello?"

"Hey." The woman smiled, her lips twisting slyly. "I live next door. Are you the new owner of this place?"

Gia forced her brain to kick into gear. "Yeah…"

"Welcome. I'm Viv." She seemed younger than Gia, maybe twenty, her short black hair gelled into an artful wave. Her outfit said she was on her way to or from the gym, and she had the biceps to match.

"Um, hi. I'm Gia." Her stomach flipped. Was it smart to give out her real name? She was well out of the Balzanos' reach, but still.

Viv crossed her arms. "Were you close to the woman who lived here before?"

Gia didn't see how it was her business. "Were you?"

"No, I haven't lived in the building long. This place was never listed for sale, so you must have known Susan Lockwood."

Why did she care? "Yeah. Sorry. I've had a long night. I was sleeping, so if you don't mind, later would be a better time to catch up."

"And if I mind?" Viv raised an eyebrow.

Gia was stunned by the sheer audacity.

"I'm kidding." Viv huffed, almost a laugh. "I'll see you around." She turned and disappeared into the neighboring condo.

Gia shut the door and locked it. Hopefully, Viv wasn't part of the Lockwood Coven.

Gia woke around sunset, the evening light filtering in through the living room windows.

She glanced outside and surveyed the street, unable to tell if any of the parked cars contained her father's men, staking out her building. There were no shiny black SUVs, at least.

Gia might be paranoid, but her escape had been too easy. Her father's men should have caught up to her.

Once they saw her leaving on the back alley camera, all they'd had to do was ask one of the businesses around the corner for their street footage, and they'd have found the car she'd escaped in. Yeah, Sam had driven like a possessed woman, but the Balzanos wouldn't have had to stop in their pursuit. They could have swapped drivers.

Maybe the Balzanos hadn't figured out where Sam had gone after getting on the highway. Maybe they thought Gia had gone south. Or fled to Canada. She had her passport with her, and her father had probably searched her room by now and realized it was missing.

The big question was: had Franco known where his wife

and her lover had been trying to take Gia all those years ago, and was he aware of Jeffrey's surviving family?

Even if Franco hadn't known about Susan before, he could figure out Jeffrey had a sister and track Gia down. But then, Franco had no idea Gia had discovered her true parentage. He didn't know why she'd run. His mind wouldn't immediately go to Jeffrey Lockwood.

But it wasn't smart to stay here.

Gia needed to sell the condo and the theater and move somewhere *she* wanted to live. There was no reason to stay in the place she'd been brought by some random lawyer and his coven.

The beginnings of a plan motivated Gia to step away from the window and do something more productive than watch the street. She had to get moving if she wanted to turn this unexpected inheritance into a real future.

Gia divided her cash between a cereal box—the kitchen was stocked with a few basics—the cupboard housing the water heater, and the gap behind the washing machine. With a stack of twenties in her pocket, she left the condo.

Surprisingly, Gia felt refreshed. Her headache was gone, which was a win right there. Frankly, getting through the cross-country trip without an episode was a miracle, but she wouldn't question her good luck.

She wandered the neighborhood until she found a corner store and bought a new phone and prepaid SIM. The old one went in the nearest trash can.

Gia didn't bother to save Ramirez's number, planning find her own lawyer to handle the sales of her newly acquired assets.

After stopping to eat a burrito at a little hole-in-the-wall restaurant, Gia returned the way she'd come.

She paused outside her building, attention on the dark theater across the street. According to Rameriez, there weren't any productions on at the moment, and the old movie screenings that usually happened on weekends ceased when Susan passed away.

The Spotlight Theater had a classic look, and the building could easily be as old as the others on the block, but the paint looked relatively fresh. The marquee was blank, and the posters on either side of the doors were half taken down, leaving ripped remnants advertising the last show, but otherwise the place seemed far from abandoned.

Gia sifted through her keys, trying each one until she unlocked the front door.

Night had fallen, and she fumbled around inside for the lights. Once she could see, she closed and locked the front door behind her before surveying her new business.

The vintage vibe extended into the building's interior, with worn red carpet beneath her feet and grand embellishments along the walls and ceiling. Everything seemed well cared for, the building's old features preserved rather than modernized. To one side sat a ticket counter and concession stand. Opposite, loomed a well-lit stairwell, and the center of the far wall housed closed double doors.

Gia pushed one of the doors open.

It was dark, and she could hardly make out the stage beyond the rows of seats. Gia didn't feel like searching for the lights, so she closed the door and headed up the stairs.

A hall to one side led to balcony seating. In the other direction, she found a line of closed doors, which seemed more promising. Hopefully, Susan had an office around here since there had been nothing related to the theater at the condo.

Gia needed to go over the theater's expenses and income and figure out its net worth. She'd studied business in college and wasn't worried about doing a little analysis. Sure, she wasn't very knowledgeable about theaters in particular, but she could learn, and if all else failed, she could scrap the business and sell the property on its own.

With the lights flicked on, Gia worked her way along the hall. She found restrooms and the projection control room. It was too bad the theater hadn't stayed open after her aunt's death and kept screening old movies. That way, it could have received some income.

Had all the employees lost their jobs?

Even if the business had been profitable, Gia didn't know if she could revive it after the closure and get everything going again. At least not before she needed to move on from Shearwater Landing.

The last door in the hallway was locked, and Gia sifted through the keys, trying them one at a time until at last, the lock clicked.

A chill ran down Gia's spine, but a look over her shoulder reassured her she was alone. Maybe that was the problem. A creepy sensation she hadn't noticed before seemed to settle over everything.

But Gia had been raised better than to be afraid of the dark.

People were dangerous, not deserted old theaters, and no mention of covens or witches—or anything superstitious—would prevent Gia from taking this opportunity and turning it into freedom from the Balzanos.

Gia opened the door, finding the inside dark. No surprise there. She ran her hand along the wall, flipped the light switch, and walked into the room.

Ice enveloped her, like an arctic wind hitting out of nowhere. Gia gasped, her chest tight.

What the fuck?

She sucked in air, clutching her sweater above her heart, and spun around, her skin prickling.

There, between her and the door, was a ghost.

EIGHT

AURORA

THE LIGHTS in the room came on, and a woman walked through the door.

Through Aurora.

A light tingling sensation overwhelmed her. *Hey! I thought that wasn't possible,* Aurora fumed to herself, outraged by her inconsistent ability to move through solid objects.

But fuck, it didn't matter. A person was here.

Had the woman felt their contact? She spun around and froze, her tanned complexion going pale.

"Can you see me?" Aurora asked out loud. Or at least, she hoped it was out loud, given she had no body with which to produce sound.

The woman stumbled backward and hit the desk, her hand fluttering to cover her mouth.

So she *could* see Aurora. Excellent.

Aurora drifted closer. "Can you hear me?"

The woman whimpered, her eyes so wide the whites were visible all the way around. She smelled sweet and almost familiar. How Aurora could smell in ghost-form, she didn't know. It wasn't as if she'd picked up on any other scents in the room, and she'd been here a while.

She did her best to look non-threatening.

The woman closed her eyes, muttering, "No. It can't be a ghost." Then reopened them, her long lashes fluttering.

Aurora waved. "Obviously, you can see me, but if you can hear me, I'd appreciate you letting me—"

The woman screamed and launched forward, crashing through Aurora and filling her ghostly body with electric tingles.

Aurora spun in time to see the woman fumbling with the door.

"Wait!" Aurora yelled, swooping forward.

The door slammed in her face, and she crashed into it.

"Fuck!" Aurora pounded her translucent fists against the door, but she still didn't know if the woman could hear her.

Running footsteps pattered away, the sound growing faint. Aurora stilled and strained to listen. A few moments later, there was the distant sound of a slamming door.

"Satan damn you." Aurora kicked the door, the muted ache in her ghostly toe adding to her ire.

When it was clear no one was returning in a hurry, Aurora faced the room. Her prison. The woman had left the light on. Aurora hadn't noticed it being dark before. It seemed ghosts could see pretty well regardless.

Okay. This wasn't all bad. Aurora had never seen that woman before in her life, and hadn't gotten a good look out the door, but it wasn't the end of the world.

Surely someone would return.

Wherever Aurora was, it wasn't abandoned. She'd wait and do a better job of not scaring the next person who came by.

Aurora settled on the desk, and time stretched agonizingly slow.

With no windows, she couldn't count how many days had passed since she'd arrived, and she didn't seem to experience fatigue in this form. It warped her perception. Minutes and hours all felt the same.

Fuck, she had to get out of here.

Sometime later, a thought occurred. Was it possible to make herself invisible so the next person didn't run off so quickly?

Strictly speaking, a witch couldn't create an illusion strong enough to render themself invisible, but Aurora was in uncharted territory here. She had no sense of her magic and couldn't cast spells. All her active power must've still been running through her blood in her body, meaning she'd miscalculated when putting this spell together... But perhaps there was another way to harness the magic in her soul.

Even if she couldn't access her usual abilities, magic ruled her existence in this form. A soul was pure magic. How else could she speak, hear, and feel with no vocal cords, ears, or nerves? Even if the jury was out on whether she could be heard by others, she could be seen.

But what if she simply didn't want to be seen?

Raising a hand in front of her face, Aurora told herself to be invisible. Nothing happened. She scowled and tried again, meditating on the idea of going unnoticed. Willing her presence to be missed.

She opened her eyes, and her hand was gone.

Aurora wiggled her finger and saw nothing. She brought her hand to her nose, feeling along her face, but still didn't see anything in front of her.

It was thrilling. Aurora knew the bounds of her magic better than almost anything, and to discover something new, something completely outside the realm of what she'd believed possible, made her wonder what else she could do.

The echo of a closing door sounded in the distance.

Aurora jolted, her hand flickering into view. She drifted to the corner of the room and willed herself to go unnoticed, tingles of anticipation twisting inside her.

Footsteps sounded outside. There was a pause, then the handle turned.

The door flung open and crashed into the wall.

The same woman with dark brown hair appeared in the doorway. Her eyes narrowed, and she scanned the room.

She huffed. "There's nothing here."

She didn't sound entirely confident, but Aurora wasn't about to reveal herself. With another look around, the woman shut the door and stepped farther into the office.

It was annoying that she hadn't left it open. Oh well. She'd have to leave eventually, and Aurora would sneak out with her.

Mystery-woman tucked her hair behind her ears, opened a filing cabinet, and rifled through a few folders, a frown tugging at her soft pink lips. With a sigh, she closed the cabinet and sat behind the desk to turn on the computer, typing in the password written on a sticky note stuck to the monitor.

The woman's brow furrowed as she scanned the computer screen.

If Aurora had to guess, whoever-she-was was in her mid-twenties, same as Aurora. Reflexively, Aurora scanned her for magic, but without direct access to her own power, the detection spell didn't work.

How frustrating. Aurora had no clue if this woman was a witch, vampire, or human.

As the mystery woman clicked around on the computer, Aurora drifted out of her corner. Unnoticed, she hovered behind her companion's shoulder and snooped on the screen.

Eww. Spreadsheets.

The file window closed, revealing a picture of the Spotlight Theater as the desktop background.

Aurora's invisible skin prickled. Was *that* where she was?

It almost made sense.

No wonder no one had been around while she'd moldered away in this office for Satan knew how long. Susan Lockwood had passed away, and Aurora had heard the theater was closed while the coven grieved.

Aurora had met the Lockwood Coven leader once, when Susan had officially invited her to join. Of course, Susan's death had delayed Aurora accepting, but she hadn't wanted to bother any of her friends about coven membership when their loss was fresh. It wasn't like the offer would disappear once the witches had selected a new leader, and Aurora couldn't officially join until she'd left her coven. She'd been busy trying to gather the courage to sever her earthly ties, arguing with her friends about there being no other way.

Something about the Lockwood Coven's offer to join their ranks must have drawn her soul. Hopefully, it was a sign she was on the right track. On a path to the better life she'd always dreamed of.

A surge of hope filled Aurora, and she drifted higher into the air. It was too bad one of her friends hadn't walked in and found her.

Wait. If this mystery woman was part of the Lockwood Coven, why had she been so scared?

Souls didn't leave their bodies and linger in this realm, but most witches and vampires would be curious about a ghost's existence rather than terrified.

Was this lady human? An *unaware* human?

Whoever she was, she seemed intent on going through every single file on the computer. If Aurora weren't worried about scaring her off, she'd have told her to hurry up.

When the computer files were exhausted, the woman started flipping through each logbook in the desk.

What was she looking for?

The woman froze, page mid-turn, and slowly looked over her shoulder. Fear lit her dark brown eyes, but she didn't look at Aurora. Her gaze landed to the left. Could she feel Aurora watching? Slowly, she returned to the logbook. Instead of continuing to flip through it, she closed it and stacked the others on top.

Aurora zipped over to the door.

As soon as the woman opened it, logbooks bundled under her arm, Aurora shot out of the room.

She was indeed in the Spotlight Theater. Aurora didn't stop to take it in as she zoomed down the stairs, stopping short at the closed front doors.

Damn.

Aurora waited impatiently for the mystery woman to join her.

She appeared, unlocked and opened the door, and Aurora shot forward.

A strong tug took hold of her midsection, and she halted in mid-air, right on the threshold.

"What the fuck!" Aurora struggled forward to no avail. What was keeping her here?

A shrill scream pierced Aurora's ears.

Seemed she wasn't invisible any longer. But that wasn't her biggest concern. Was there a boundary spell sealing off the building? Why couldn't she leave?

Aurora gave in and screamed.

"Oh my god, please don't hurt me."

Aurora spun around. The woman backed away, looking almost ill with fear, logbooks falling to the floor as her hands trembled.

"Hey." Aurora raised her hands in surrender. "I won't hurt you. I need your help."

The woman swallowed, and her next words were soft. "My —my help?"

Aurora smiled. "So you *can* hear me."

The woman's face closed off, hardening into a steel barrier. "You're my hallucination. Of course I can hear you."

Aurora floated slightly closer. "I'm not a hallucination. I'm real. Please, I need you to tell the Lockwood Coven that Aurora Thornfield is trapped here."

"The Lockwood Coven?" The woman let out a bitter laugh. "Is that where the idea for this stupid vision came from? One lawyer blabs about witches, and I lose my mind?" She frowned. "Oh god, what if I've passed out and this is a new symptom?"

Aurora had no clue what she was talking about. "You aren't passed out. You're talking to me right now. Please. You have to help me."

"No. *I* need help."

If this woman thought she was talking to an imaginary person, this would go nowhere. Aurora changed tactics. "Maybe I can help you. What's your name?"

She hesitated for a long moment, a lock of hair falling into her face, but she didn't brush it aside. "Gia," she said at last.

Aurora liked the name, short and punchy. "Nice to meet you. I'm Aurora."

"Um...hi?" Gia's lips twitched, and she almost smiled.

"Hi." Aurora floated closer, and Gia didn't retreat.

Their eyes locked, and a tingle vibrated through Aurora's soul. When she wasn't scared out of her mind, Gia's delicate face was as sweet as her scent.

The moment passed too quickly, and Gia closed her eyes, making a helpless sound. "Ghosts aren't real. Covens aren't real. Witches aren't real." She fixed Aurora with a glare. "*You* aren't real."

So Gia was a human, unaware of the magic world. But

then… "If witches aren't real, how do you know the Lockwood Coven?"

Gia's expression darkened, her knuckles turning white as she gripped the only logbook she hadn't dropped. "Knowing someone in a cult doesn't make witches real. How can you be real? I can see through you."

Aurora's frustration flared, or maybe it was something darker. "If I'm not real, why are you talking to me?"

Gia seemed to deflate, and she averted her eyes. "I don't know. So I don't have to be alone."

Aurora's phantom heart clenched. "Funny. I don't want to be alone either."

There was a long silence, but Aurora couldn't think of a single thing to say. All the hopelessness she'd felt the night she'd lain down in the dirt to take this risky stab at freedom swelled within her.

"I'm sorry. I have to go." Gia skirted around Aurora. "God, why am I explaining myself? You aren't even really here."

"No, wait!" Aurora followed her to the door, but Gia didn't stop as she hurried out.

Aurora couldn't pass the threshold, the tugging sensation holding her firmly in place. "Please tell the Lockwood Coven I'm here!"

The door shut and the lock clicked. Aurora was alone.

NINE

GIA

GIA'S HEART pounded as she hurried across the street and into her condo.

She'd been talking to a ghost. No, to *herself*. She shouldn't even consider the possibility that ghosts were real.

Gia dumped the logbook on the coffee table and curled onto the couch, bending her legs and tucking them against her chest. One of her pill bottles sat on the table beside her. Too bad they didn't prevent hallucinations.

God, her stomach hurt. What was she supposed to do?

She'd been to countless doctors ever since her blackouts started, and none had come up with a conclusive explanation for what was happening. Would these hallucinations help a new doctor find a better solution for her than the pills that worked as often as they didn't? Or was she back at square one?

Gia buried her head in her hands.

She didn't need this. Physically, she could have sworn she'd been doing well. She hadn't blacked out since before escaping her family. Nothing more than a regular headache had bothered her, and since she'd recovered from the long drive, she hadn't even had a twinge.

If it weren't for the ghostly hallucinations, she'd have said she was doing better than ever.

Could they be unrelated to her headaches?

Could the ghost be *real*? Would that be so bad?

Aurora hadn't been frightening. It wasn't as if she'd been covered in blood or trying to attack Gia. If, against all odds, the ghost was real, she didn't seem more threatening than any random woman Gia might meet.

Maybe she should have given Aurora a chance to speak before running away.

If Aurora was real, and that was a big if. She probably wasn't.

Gia only entertained the idea because hallucinations were the scariest possible option, and given her luck, the worst-case scenario would turn out to be the truth. It figured she'd imagine a gorgeous woman. She was so lonely that she was being haunted by the idea of a girlfriend. Seriously, fuck her life.

A shiver wound down Gia's spine, and the hairs on her arms rose. Had the room gotten colder?

"Oh shit!" a voice shouted.

Gia's head whipped up.

The ghost was floating in the middle of her living room.

"How did I get here?" Aurora asked.

How was Gia supposed to know? She shrugged, intrigued by her own lack of fear as her goosebumps faded. She was almost relieved to see Aurora again. "I don't know. You tell me."

The ghost crossed her translucent arms and regarded Gia, her hair floating around her face as it might if she were underwater. "Is this your house?"

"Sort of. I just moved in."

Aurora spun around, her hair flowing gracefully behind her. "Well, this makes no sense."

Gia stood from the couch. "Me moving makes no sense? You existing makes no sense."

Arguing with a figment of her imagination was the real nonsense.

Aurora's attention sharpened, even as her whole form seemed to flicker in and out of focus. "What I mean is, being trapped at the theater had some logic to it. I don't get why I'd suddenly be here."

"You don't know how you got here?" Expecting the equivalent of an imaginary friend to explain anything was ridiculous, but Gia couldn't seem to help herself.

Aurora drifted to the window and peered out. "Doesn't look like I went far. I was trapped in the theater for ages, then there was this pull, and I appeared here."

Interesting, however…not as interesting as Aurora's floating hair. It was mesmerizing. Ethereal. Strands of washed-out, almost white blonde flowing in constant, gradual motion, like they were caught in a current. The ends were so translucent, Gia could hardly make them out as they swayed.

What would Aurora's hair feel like? Each lock appeared silky soft, but Gia's hand would sadly pass right through.

And the rest of Aurora… Gia had to employ every strategy she'd learned over a lifetime of not openly gawking at women for fear of making them uncomfortable. She wanted to do nothing but stare at Aurora, and really shouldn't.

Well, maybe not *nothing*, but she was keeping her thoughts appropriate.

Yet she noted each one of Aurora's curves. How her bralette hugged her full breasts. The way the ghostly fabric of her sheer, mesh top clung to her shoulders and stomach, somehow giving off the same white sheen as her skin, while still conveying the undertones of color.

Gia's imagination could ensnare her all right. This ghost

was gorgeous, and her modern appearance almost tempted Gia into believing she was real.

Aurora turned away from the window, and Gia's face heated. "What were you doing at the theater?"

"Getting a handle on the business. Did you say you were trapped there?" Had Aurora died in the theater? She couldn't have if she were a hallucination, but still, Gia's heart ached at the thought.

"I'm in the process of joining the Lockwood Coven, so the connection must have drawn me in and trapped me. But what does that have to do with you? Are you part of the coven?"

Gia's stomach flipped. "I have nothing to do with any coven."

Aurora floated closer, and Gia took a stumbling step away. Aurora stopped abruptly. "You've got something to do with the Lockwoods if you were in the theater."

"No, I don't. Look, I don't even know if you're real."

Aurora huffed like she couldn't believe they'd returned to this ridiculous argument. "I'll prove I'm real, okay? You know *someone* in the Lockwood Coven. Otherwise, you couldn't have gotten inside the theater. Call whoever it is and ask if Aurora Thornfield requested to join."

Gia didn't want to talk to Ramirez. Asking about his coven would encourage him to recruit her, and she needed a coven in her life like she needed a hole in the head.

Unless... Oh fuck, she was losing it, but she couldn't help wondering: if Aurora was real, could *witches* be real? Magic and spells, and who the hell knew what else?

Gia changed her mind. That was the worst-case scenario. She'd rather deal with hallucinations.

"*Please.*" Aurora drifted even closer, her features twisted in desperation. "I need your help."

Aurora's pain seemed to fill the air, and Gia swore the

feeling echoed her own, the familiarity crushing. How could she deny helping someone? She was only here because of the kindness of strangers.

"Okay. I'll call."

Aurora shimmered, her expression relaxing. "Thank you."

Gia's stomach twisted. She didn't deserve gratitude. Averting her eyes, she curled onto the couch and grabbed her phone to look up Edward Ramirez, Shearwater Landing lawyer.

Aurora hovered at the other end of the couch, her arms crossed. As if pulled by a magnetic force, Gia met her stare, unable to look away as she raised the ringing phone to her ear.

She was either about to sound ridiculous or confirm something she wasn't sure she truly wanted to know.

"Ramirez Legal Services, this is Grace. How can I help?"

"Hi. I was in to see Mr. Ramirez the other day and had a… uh… follow-up question. My name is Gia." She didn't want to give her last time to this unknown receptionist, or Aurora. They might not have heard of the Balzanos all the way out here, but she couldn't shake her cautionary nature.

"Oh, *Gia*," Grace said, recognition brightening her tone. "Edward will be pleased you called. I'll pop you through."

The line went quiet. Seemed Grace was already aware of who she was. Made sense, but unease put Gia on alert. Was Grace part of the coven?

"What can I do for you, Gia?" Ramirez's familiar voice asked.

She cleared her throat. "I have a question about the coven you mentioned."

He hummed, sounding pleased. "Of course. Ask away. You're welcome to come over in person and—"

"No, that's not necessary. I was wondering if Aurora Thornfield requested to join?"

"Do you know Aurora?" Surprise lit Ramirez's tone.

Gia's grip tightened on her phone. Holy shit. "Do *you*?"

"Not personally. I believe Aurora is close friends with Lilly and some of the younger witches. I look after our official membership records. Susan was coordinating Aurora Thornfield's acceptance into the coven before her death. I really should follow up."

"Awesome. Thanks. Bye." Gia cringed and ended the call.

Aurora raised a brow. "So?"

"He said you were joining the coven."

"And if I were a figment of your imagination, there'd be no way for him to know what you were talking about. You couldn't randomly guess the name of someone joining the Lockwood Coven."

Shit, she was right. Gia's heart thumped, her pulse rushing in her ears. Ghosts were real, and her aunt had been in a coven. Of real witches.

What had Gia gotten herself into?

"Don't panic." A small smile tugged on Aurora's lips. "This is good."

"No, it isn't. I need to get away from these people. I'm done living a life controlled by power-hungry mobs."

Confusion broke over Aurora's face, her form flickering. "The Lockwoods aren't after power. Do you know other witches like that?"

"I don't know any other witches. I didn't believe they were real until five seconds ago."

"Right." Aurora shook herself, her hair swirling. "How'd you find the Lockwood Coven, anyway?"

"I didn't. They found me."

Aurora snorted as if she didn't believe her any more than Gia first believed in ghosts. "They found you and gave you keys to the Spotlight Theater out of nowhere?"

"What does the theater have to do with anything? My aunt owned it, and I inherited it. It's mine now."

Aurora's eyes widened. "Susan Lockwood was your *aunt*?"

Damn it. Gia didn't want to share personal information, but at the same time, she needed answers. Maybe Aurora could explain who these Lockwood people actually were.

"Yeah, Susan was my aunt, but I didn't know her. I discovered our connection recently. Turns out, I'm not as related to the father I grew up with as I thought."

"But you're related to Susan, by blood?" Aurora's gaze slid over Gia.

Her skin prickled as if she'd been touched, and she bit her lip. Oh, dear lord, she needed to focus. Aurora was *not* checking her out.

Aurora's assessing stare turned triumphant. "So you *are* a witch."

A flare of indignation scorched through Gia. "No, I'm not. I'm..." She didn't know what the word for not-a-witch was, but she knew who *she* was. And she wasn't a witch.

"Human?" Aurora suggested.

"Yes. Exactly." Gia was human. Of-fucking-course she was.

Aurora seemed to come to some conclusion and smiled, the gesture maddeningly placating. *See*, definitely not checking her out. Aurora probably thought Gia was clueless.

"I hear you," Aurora said soothingly, like Gia was five. "You aren't part of the Lockwood Coven—or any coven—which makes sense if you're human, but you can still help me. I need to see if I can get out of this building."

"Why do you need my help for that?"

Aurora's voice tightened. "Because I can't open doors or move physical objects."

Was that really all Aurora needed? Someone to open the door? Gia squashed a swell of disappointment. "If I open the door for you, will you tell me what the deal is with your coven before you go?"

A shadow passed over Aurora's translucent face, making her hard to see for a split second. "My coven? Oh. You mean the Lockwoods? Sure. Open the window for me, and I promise I'll tell you, but I need to know if I'm trapped first. I'm on a bit of a time crunch, so I might need to answer your questions later."

Gia wanted an explanation now, but it was wrong to keep Aurora trapped. Gia knew that more than most.

She stood and went to the window. Where could a ghost possibly be hurrying off to? The afterlife? The thought sent a stab of remorse through Gia. It would have been nice to be friends with Aurora if she were alive.

An image of a fiery pit popped into Gia's mind. Nope. She did not want to think about the potential realities of Hell right now.

She glanced down at the street, her hand on the window latch, and hesitated at the sight of a man standing in front of the theater, frowning at her building. Gia's heart skipped.

After a closer look, she was sure she'd never seen the guy before. Her father wouldn't send anyone but his most trusted men after her. Besides, he didn't know where she was. She was being paranoid. People glared at buildings all the time. Maybe he thought it was ugly.

Gia unlatched the window, and Aurora appeared at her elbow. The ghost gasped, and ice enveloped Gia's wrist.

She pulled her hand away from the latch and whirled around, but no one was there. The room was completely empty. "H-hello?"

"I'm here," hissed Aurora's disembodied voice. "Don't open the window. I know that guy."

He was still lingering across the street, and Gia swore he was looking right at her window.

She quickly stepped out of sight.

"Fuck." Aurora reappeared on the other side of the room, her form flickering in and out of focus as she glided back and forth, one hand tangled in her hair. "How did they know I was here? They can't track me. All my blood is in my body!"

Gia grimaced. "Blood?"

Aurora froze and gave Gia a look, like she'd forgotten she was there.

Gia pretended that didn't sting.

"Never mind my blood. He's from my coven. Not the Lockwoods, the coven I'm trying to escape. Fuck!"

Gia crossed the room, the urge to comfort Aurora nearly overwhelming. *Aurora was trying to escape, too?* Of all the things to have in common with a ghost. "What do you mean escape? Aren't you, um, dead?"

Aurora shook her head like Gia was spouting nonsense. "I'm not dead."

But she was a ghost. She couldn't be alive. Was it rude to argue? Gia wasn't about to tell someone else who they were, but *come on.*

"If I were dead, I wouldn't be here on Earth," Aurora continued, calm as can be, like she was explaining something utterly mundane. "Earth is for the living. Dead witches go to the Realm of the Damned, which wasn't my aim. I've vacated my body temporarily, and I need to retrieve it. But if Trey is here—"

"Sorry. Realm of the Damned?"

Aurora ignored the question. "You'll have to help me open the crypt. My coven won't have left me in the woods, and they've obviously found me. I mean, it's been days. Weeks? Damnation. What if they've realized I'm not dead? If they're looking for me, who knows where they've stashed my body."

This was taking a turn for the horrific. Gia shouldn't have been so quick to assume helping Aurora wouldn't be some macabre quest because she wasn't gruesome or overtly murderous.

A lightheadedness threatened Gia's consciousness, and she gripped the couch for support. "I never agreed to open a crypt for you. A door. A window. Sure. But I'm not defiling a grave site. I don't even know what the fuck you're talking about! What do you mean *Realm of the Damned?*"

Gia could not handle finding out Hell was real. She'd explode with rage at the sheer injustice.

Aurora went completely still, finally picking up on Gia's frayed nerves. "You're right. Sorry. It would be far easier if you knew...anything, but lack of knowledge isn't your fault."

"Hey. I know things." Gia knew a hell of a lot more than the average person, thank you very much. Laundering money? Check. Disposing of a body? Check. What illegal substance provided the best profit margins? Check.

She hadn't been directly involved in her father's empire, but she'd been paying attention, and Marc wasn't as good at keeping things from her as he thought.

"I'm sure you do," Aurora said in that placating tone. "But you don't know about magic, which is what we're dealing with."

Gia's indignation fizzled out. "Yeah, well, magic wasn't supposed to be real; otherwise, I would have studied up."

Aurora's face flickered, her lips twitching in a gorgeous smile. "Why don't I fill you in?"

TEN

AURORA

IT TURNED OUT, Aurora had been trapped in the Spotlight Theater for nearly two weeks, which was too long any way she looked at it. The bright side? She wasn't trapped anymore, and they'd cleared up her real-or-not status.

It was the bare minimum, but it was all Aurora had.

"What do you mean you were bound to your coven?" Gia asked.

Aurora wasn't withholding any information. Hopefully, the more Gia understood, the more willing she'd be to do as Aurora asked.

"I couldn't physically leave if they didn't allow it, and my magic was useless against them. They controlled me more completely than even the most domineering human could imagine."

Gia's expression was appropriately horrified, her eyes wide. "And they have your *body*?" She still sounded unconvinced that Aurora was alive.

Aurora had explained the afterlife, human reincarnation, witches' damnation—no, Hell was not what Gia had been taught in Sunday school—and how all this meant she couldn't possibly be dead. But upon hearing all this, Gia had had no response except to stare at Aurora in silent relief, like a woman who'd been told all her life that she'd go to a human version of Hell.

Understandably, she hadn't latched onto the logic in Aurora's argument.

The stony way she'd digested the truth of the afterlife compared to what she'd been taught was impressive, but not the point Aurora needed her focused on, no matter how monumental it might be. Not when Aurora couldn't escape the feeling she was running out of time.

Her body was suspended by magic, preserved in a state that could survive untouched for months, but her mortal flesh was vulnerable.

"I wasn't supposed to leave my body behind." Aurora couldn't help sounding defensive. "I was only meant to be a soul for a second, but something called me to the theater, and I couldn't fight it."

"And you think your intention to join the Lockwood Coven called you?" Gia repeated what Aurora had told her earlier with no small amount of skepticism.

Aurora didn't blame her. Without official ties to the Lockwoods, she had her own doubts and no explanation for why she'd been called to Gia's apartment.

"It doesn't really matter how I got to the theater. Getting into the crypt to retrieve my body would have been hard enough if my family had taken me for dead. The property is warded, for one. But they've tracked me here somehow, so they might be expecting me. We need reinforcements."

"How about you do your invisibility thing, I'll open the window, and you can zoom off to the Lockwoods for backup?"

"What if Trey captures me when I go outside?" Ice rippled through Aurora, and she shuddered.

She had no clue what her coven could do to her in this form. Being free of their ties didn't mean she wasn't vulnerable, especially with no ability to use active magic and cast spells. Not understanding what pulled her from one place to another meant there was no guarantee she was safe. The Thornfields could find a way to ensnare her.

They might find a way to rebind her to the coven.

Gia didn't seem to have a response, so Aurora pressed on. "You need to ask the Lockwoods for help and tell them what's happening before I do anything else."

"But I don't want to be involved with them." Gia was oddly desperate to avoid the Lockwoods, and Aurora couldn't help the frustration welling inside her.

Gia didn't seem to realize she was already involved with the coven, whether she liked it or not. Susan had been her aunt. Her family. Her blood. The Lockwoods didn't enforce loyalty like the Thornfields, meaning Gia could walk away, but she couldn't pretend the coven had nothing to do with her.

Even without being able to sense it, Aurora was sure Gia had magical power of her own. She was a witch by blood and had a place in the Lockwood Coven if she chose. She'd inherited their headquarters, for Satan's sake.

Why Susan left her estate to someone unaware was a mystery Aurora didn't need right now.

Gia rubbed her temple. She stood, grabbed a bottle from the side table, and popped a pill into her mouth. "I'm starving, and it's giving me a headache, so I'm going to grab some food at the deli around the corner. You can stay here or fly off to the Lockwoods for help. Okay?"

Aurora shot to her side. "Wait. You can't leave."

Gia's gentle features hardened, her glare surprisingly cold. "Are you going to stop me?"

Aurora was taken aback by her biting tone. "No. I didn't mean it like that."

A pause. "Sorry. You're not the only one who has a controlling family." Warmth returned to Gia's expression. "I know you need help, and I want to help you, believe me. But what can I do? I can't use magic. I can't protect you from Trey or help you sneak into the Thornfield compound, and it's not like you're safe in here if he's found you. Why wait around, getting me involved? Go find the Lockwoods so they can protect you. You don't need me."

Even if Gia was a witch and didn't know it, she had a point. Gia had no clue how to use magic. She'd be no match for anyone, and Trey could break in at any moment.

Then why didn't Aurora want to go? Had being locked in the theater alone scarred her that badly?

She pushed the thought away. "All right. I'll follow you outside and go find the Lockwoods. Thanks for getting me out of the theater." Aurora told herself that escaping her confines was more than enough help from Gia. For some reason, she didn't believe it.

"No problem. At least now I know my aunt wasn't in a creepy cult. I'd never have figured out who the Lockwoods were on my own."

She would have if she'd accepted Edward's offer to explain, rather than avoid him as she'd admitted to doing. Instead of pointing this out Aurora found herself saying, "If you have more questions, I can answer them some other time."

Gia hesitated for the briefest moment, her expression unreadable. "Sure." She grabbed an oversized hoodie off the couch and pulled it over her head, leaving hair tangled around her face as she emerged.

Aurora forgot what she'd been about to say. She swore she could feel the static electricity clinging to Gia's hair from across the room. Which was wild. The little zaps shot through her ghostly form, and she shuddered.

Gia huffed in annoyance—oblivious to the charge electrifying Aurora's soul—and cleared her face, a few stray strands persistently sticking to her forehead. An air of exhaustion settled over her, and the electricity dissipated.

Guilt replaced the swirls of excitement coursing through Aurora. She shouldn't abandon Gia after dumping so much on her. But what choice did she have? Gia would still be here once Aurora retrieved her body.

After escaping her coven once and for all, Aurora would make sure Gia adjusted to the reality of the magic world. And when Aurora had her body, she could help Gia tame her beautiful wavy hair, perhaps pull it into a braid.

If Gia wanted.

"So, are you going to turn invisible?" Gia asked.

Woops. Aurora had been staring. "Yep." She willed herself to be unnoticed.

"Great. Follow me."

Gia left the apartment and headed down the stairs, Aurora gliding unseen behind her.

Through the ground floor window, Trey was visible, lurking by the theater and looking at his phone. Gia pressed the lock release, exiting the building, and Aurora slipped out behind her.

Trey's head snapped up, and he scowled at Gia before returning his attention to the phone. Had he sensed Aurora's presence? Was such a thing possible? Trey wasn't doing any obvious magic, but without the ability to cast a detection spell, Aurora couldn't be sure he wasn't using a silent spell.

There was no point lingering. Aurora shot into the sky, and Gia headed down the street. Trey didn't give any indication he'd noticed Aurora's departure, instead refocusing on Gia.

Good, he was distracted, and Lilly's apartment wasn't far away. Aurora flew over the top of the theater and paused, unable to help looking down one last time. Gia crossed the street, her pace unhurried.

Should Aurora have said more of a goodbye?

An unexpected ache filled her as the woman moved farther away...but no. This wasn't the time. She'd find Gia after—

The ache inside her exploded, turning into a gut-wrenching pull, clawing at the depths of her soul. The next instant, Aurora was on the sidewalk beside Gia.

Aurora glanced around frantically. "What the hell?"

Gia nearly tripped over her feet. She recovered and kept moving. "Aurora? Are you still here?"

At least she'd remained invisible. "Yeah. I tried to leave, but it didn't work."

Gia pursed her lips and kept walking.

Aurora didn't follow. She shot into the sky and away from Gia, but she didn't even make it to the theater before her soul ached, and she appeared at Gia's side.

No. This could not be happening.

Was she tied *to Gia*? Why? That shouldn't be possible.

Gia glanced around uneasily and ducked into the deli. Aurora didn't bother slipping inside after her.

Fuck this. Aurora managed to keep the words in her head, her desire to be unnoticed as strong as ever, but she could easily have screamed. If Gia hadn't been so obviously unaware of witches and everything magical, Aurora would have sworn she'd done something to trap her.

Movement at the street corner caught Aurora's attention, and she turned to where Trey lingered, pacing like he was waiting for someone.

Had he sensed Aurora's spirit and followed?

No. He gave no sign of recognition, and surely, if he could tell Aurora was floating here unseen, he'd be doing something to capture her.

Aurora pressed against the building and waited helplessly, fear coiling inside her, but Trey did nothing.

Eventually, the deli door swung open, and Gia exited, a large paper bag clutched to her chest. She didn't pause or look around as she strode purposefully in the direction of home.

Aurora followed. She had no choice. If she didn't trail along, it seemed she'd be pulled to Gia's side regardless. At least with Gia in earshot, she didn't feel like she'd be spirited away by her coven and never heard from again.

Gia glanced over her shoulder as she rounded the corner, her gaze casually landing on Trey, who stood across the street. The paper bag crunched under Gia's fingers, but her demeanor didn't change as she continued walking. Had she not realized it was the same man who'd been outside her building?

A few moments after leaving Trey behind, he rounded the corner, his gaze fixed on Gia, clearly following.

But he couldn't be. Why would he follow Gia?

Aurora floated as far away from Gia as she could without triggering the aching feeling, but Trey didn't react. His attention remained solely on the other woman.

Hollow dread weighed Aurora down. Whatever this meant, it couldn't be good.

The now-familiar tug on her soul cut through her sinking thoughts, and she zipped to Gia's side just as she reentered her building. The lock clicked behind them as the door shut.

As soon as she was in the stairwell, Gia's face fell, her forehead creasing.

Aurora couldn't help her smile. "So you did notice him following? You hid it well."

Gia's steps faltered, and she glared slightly to the right of where Aurora was hidden. "You're still here? Wait, don't say anything. Let's get inside. I don't want to stand here talking to myself."

Aurora bit her lip to smother a laugh and floated up the stairs after her.

When they were in the condo, Aurora abandoned her invisibility. "Have you ever come across Trey before?"

"No." Gia set the groceries on the kitchen counter, pulled out a bag of chips, and opened it. "I've only been in Shearwater Landing for a few days."

That surprised Aurora. "Where are you from?"

Gia ate a chip and began unpacking the rest of the bag, pulling out a few small jars, a loaf of bread, something flat packed in butcher paper, and finally, what looked like a wrapped sandwich.

"I'm from Ashton Lakes," she said at last.

Aurora had heard of it, but she'd never been that far east. "Why would Trey be following you if you're from out of town and don't know about magic?"

"You tell me. I thought he was here for you. And why haven't you left? Weren't you flying off to the Lockwood Coven?"

"I can't get away from you. Every time I try, I'm pulled to your side."

Gia froze, the unwrapped sandwich halfway to her mouth. "What?"

Aurora drifted closer. "We need magical help. I don't know what's happening and can't figure it out without access to my active powers. You can't help either, since you're *human*."

Gia frowned. "Don't say it like that. I am human."

"Sure, a human who's blood relatives with a witch."

"Magic can't be hereditary." Gia snorted like Aurora was being ridiculous and dug into her food.

Damn, the sandwich looked good, bursting with lettuce and cheese. Aurora wasn't hungry, but knowing it had been weeks since she'd eaten had her longing for a taste.

"Magic is hereditary. Bloodlines are a big deal to witches like the Thornfields. Anyone whose lineage leads back to Lucifer—our Damned Lord—is revered." She rolled her eyes.

Gia sputtered, coughed, and nearly choked on her sandwich. "*Lucifer? The Devil is real? And you're related to him?*"

"Me? No. The Thornfields aren't direct descendants. Some other demon spawned us."

"*Demon?*" Gia's face paled.

"Don't worry, they're all trapped in the Realm of the Damned. And before you freak out, demons are only damned for giving birth to witches. Like I said before, it's not some Heaven and Hell hoopla. Nothing you learned about Lucifer is true either."

Gia relaxed, muttering, "Heaven and Hell hoopla," with a shake of her head. "I take it all back. I wish you were a hallucination."

Aurora caught a hint of amusement in Gia's tone and grinned, spreading her arms wide. "Sorry, babe. I'm real."

Gia glared at her, but more like she was trying not to laugh rather than she was mad. Fuck, she was adorable.

Sure enough, Gia's lips twitched into a tiny smile. "I'm not creative enough to make you up, that's for fucking sure."

A chuckle burst from Aurora, and Gia smiled wider. Energy crackled between them, lighting Aurora's soul. Could Gia feel it too?

She grabbed her sandwich and took it over to the couch, so maybe not.

Aurora longed to join her, not as a ghost but as a woman. To feel more than electricity as their arms brushed, the heat of their bodies warming the couch as they slowly moved closer together.

She shook herself. "I'm sure I don't have to tell you, but Trey tailing you is bad. My coven doesn't fuck around. I wasn't aware of any issues between the Thornfields and Lockwoods. Do you think this has something to do with Susan dying and you inheriting the theater?"

Aurora couldn't see how. The Lockwoods weren't power players. They were an inclusive coven who stayed out of the kind of shit the Thornfields pulled in their never-ending quest to worship their Damned Lord. It didn't make sense for the Thornfields to go after the Lockwood Coven, but Trey was up to something.

"I don't know," Gia said between bites.

"Let's talk to my friend Lilly and see if she knows anything. Unless there's some other reason Trey might be after you?"

Gia gave her sandwich a dirty look, seeming to hesitate. "There isn't. Let's call your friend."

Relief had Aurora floating higher off the floor. *Finally.* "I've got Lilly's number memorized, and she lives nearby. It shouldn't take her long to get here."

"Perfect. Do you think she could bring a bottle of wine when she comes? Maybe a Chianti? A glass or two would pair really well with this bullshit."

Aurora burst into laughter. Damn, comments like that were the way to her heart, or maybe in this form, she should say the way to her soul.

"You can ask Lilly to bring wine, but you might have to settle for whatever's on sale at the nearest liquor store."

"What a pity." Gia gave a long-suffering sigh and pulled out her phone. "Once I dial, can you talk to her?"

"Sure. It shouldn't be an issue. Unless you're the only one who can hear me."

"Why would I be?"

"I don't know. The same reason I can't get away from you?"

Gia opened her mouth, then abruptly closed it, a slight flush staining her cheeks. She cleared her throat. "Surely I'm not the only one who can hear you. What's Lilly's number?"

What was that blush about? Aurora almost didn't let it go, and wouldn't have if things weren't such a mess.

Hopefully, there'd be time to work out that little mystery later. It'd be more fun than the rest of this disaster.

ELEVEN
GIA

Gia called Lilly on speaker, and Aurora gave her a rundown of how she'd become a ghost, without any trouble.

See, *of course, everyone could hear Aurora.* Gia resisted pointing this out.

Aurora's story didn't make any more sense than it had the first time Gia had heard it. It was all so fantastical, but apparently, fantasy was real now. Who'd have thought Sam driving for thirty hours straight wouldn't be the weirdest thing to happen this week?

Wait... If Sam was part of the Lockwood Coven, had she used magic to keep herself going? She must have.

Magic must have helped them evade Franco's detection the night she escaped. Blocked the street security footage of Gia getting into the car, or something like that. Gia almost asked Aurora to explain if such a thing was possible, but stopped herself. Like hell was she admitting to being on the run from the Italian mob.

Aurora might understand her desperation to escape—maybe even understand her fear—but no matter how similar their situations were, the two of them weren't the same. Aurora was a good person, fighting against an evil coven as best she could, while Gia had been complicit in her family's crimes. She'd sat around for years, doing nothing, and only ran when the odds tipped ridiculously in her favor.

She wasn't honorable like Aurora, and nowhere near as daring. No matter how little Gia understood magic or wondered how a ghost was technically alive, there was no denying that Aurora's willingness to literally step out of her body was brave as fuck.

"You idiot! I told you not to do that spell!" Lilly shrieked. Seemed she didn't agree with Gia's assessment.

At least Lilly didn't question Aurora being alive. Gia gave in and let go of her skepticism, logic be damned, and a fraction of the anxiety she'd been carrying unraveled. She hadn't wanted Aurora to be dead. It would have broken her heart.

Aurora's features hardened in response to her friend's admonishment. "Circumstances changed, Lil. They were going to shackle me to some Nightingale witch. I could cope with the binding, same as ever, but a marriage... There was no time. It was the only way off the compound."

Gia's chest tightened all over again. With all the blood blood-binding shit, she shuddered to think what marriage would have meant for Aurora. No wonder leaving her body seemed like a reasonable course of action.

"Fuck..." Lilly sounded just as stricken by the news. "That's... Fuck your family. I'll be there soon. What's the address?"

For her part, Aurora didn't seem overly emotional given what she'd shared. She glanced at Gia expectantly.

Right. She rattled off the address.

"Susan's old building?" Lilly asked, surprised.

Would the coven begrudge Susan leaving everything to her?

Gia hadn't considered that. "Susan was my aunt," she said carefully. "She left the place to me."

Before Lilly had a chance to enquire further, Aurora cut in. "Be careful of Trey. He's going to spot you coming in."

"How will Trey know Lilly doesn't live here?" Gia asked, relieved they'd moved away from her backstory.

Lilly spoke up. "He won't know for sure, but he'll probably scan me for magic and realize I'm a witch."

"You can't hide your magic?"

Aurora shook her head, her ghostly hair fluffing around her. "Not easily."

"I'll be fine," Lilly assured them. "I'm good at shielding, and I know he's there. I'll be prepared. Him spotting me is safer than asking you to come to me, and having him follow."

After a quick goodbye, Lilly hung up.

"You didn't ask about the wine," Aurora said with a twitch of her lips.

Really? "It didn't feel appropriate under the circumstances."

"Your loss. I'm going to watch for Lilly out the window." Aurora vanished from sight.

"Okay," Gia said to the seemingly empty room. With nothing else to do, she stood and idly put away the items she'd bought at the deli.

Why was a member of Aurora's awful coven following *her*? Gia wasn't a Lockwood. If Trey couldn't be sure who Lilly was, how could he know anything about her? And why couldn't Aurora leave? Were they stuck together because Gia was the one who'd found her in the theater? Like finders keepers? It couldn't be that simple.

A horrible thought struck, and Gia almost dropped the jar of mustard in her hand. Was she keeping Aurora here?

Despite pushing Aurora away, Gia hadn't wanted the ghost to leave. Gia was developing an...attachment. *Not* a crush. But something. She couldn't deny she'd much rather have Aurora around than be alone. A fierce, determined woman was exactly what Gia needed, even if the last thing she wanted was to develop unrequited feelings for a ghost.

But Gia's private urge to keep Aurora around couldn't have trapped her. The things Gia wanted didn't just happen. Her desire to avoid the Lockwoods wasn't coming to fruition.

"Lilly's here," Aurora's disembodied voice announced a short time later. "Trey doesn't seem to be paying her much attention. He's already looking at his phone again." She seemed to sigh in relief even though, as a ghost, she didn't need to breathe.

The soft, airy sound sent a shiver down Gia's spine, and she did her best to ignore it. Reacting to every little thing Aurora did wasn't helping her attachment.

Soon, Lilly was knocking on the door, and Gia went to let her in, a now-visible Aurora at her elbow.

Gia opened the door, and a tall, curvy woman with brown skin smiled and introduced herself. Gia returned the pleasantries and invited Lilly inside.

Lilly's attention landed on Aurora. "Fuck, you look wild."

The ghost huffed and floated over to the couch. "It's not a look I'm planning on keeping."

"Glad to hear it." Lilly turned serious. "Your stalker noticed me, but didn't seem poised to pounce."

"I saw. Can you detect any wards on the building?" Aurora asked.

Gia shut the door.

Lilly frowned in concentration for a few moments. "No. Susan's wards must have broken when she passed away, and no one else from the coven lives here. I've never actually been inside her place before." She glanced around the bare room.

"You weren't close?" Gia asked.

Lilly shrugged. "I'm new to the coven. Relatively speaking. I've only been a Lockwood for a few years. The elders are welcoming, don't get me wrong, but I wasn't looking to get involved in leadership and didn't see them outside meetings and coven gatherings."

Interesting, but coven politics weren't the most pressing thing at the moment. "What are wards?"

Lily's brow furrowed. "They're protective spells."

Was that all she had to say? Gia hated being left in the dark. "What do they do? Protective how?"

Lilly frowned, her gaze darting to Aurora, then to Gia. "How have you never heard of wards?"

Gia's cheeks flamed. "Because as far as I was concerned, magic wasn't real this morning."

Lilly's eyes widened. "But Susan was your aunt."

Aurora floated closer to Gia, and she wished she didn't find it comforting. "Gia didn't realize she had extended relatives until recently," Aurora explained. "I told her magic is hereditary, but—"

"But it's not." Gia's whole body heated, a sweat breaking out on her palms. "I'd know if I had magic. It's not possible."

Lilly's wide-eyed stare locked on Aurora.

"I can't sense magic in this form," Aurora said as if Lilly had asked a question.

Gia's heart rate spiked as both women looked at her. "I don't have any magic, so it doesn't matter."

"I can sense magic," Lilly said way too carefully. "Gia...you do have magical power. I can feel it."

Gia swallowed a biting remark, her fists clenching. "No, I don't. Wouldn't I know if I had magic?"

"Not necessarily," Aurora said, but Gia couldn't bring herself to look at her. "Finding out later in life happens. Especially when witches are disconnected from their magical family members."

Gia's eyes itched, and her throat burned. "But if I had magic, couldn't I use it? Wouldn't I—" *Have been able to escape? Have had a better life? Stopped my father from hurting people? Stopped my headaches from ruling my life?* She choked on the unsaid words. "Wouldn't I have noticed if I had powers? Shouldn't it have been obvious? Things exploding when I was mad or something?"

"No." Lilly's shock was replaced with concern. "Magic can't do anything unless you call on it. Casting spells is intentional. You can't accidentally use magic. But if you know what to look for, you can find it within yourself. Witches learn to tap into their power from childhood."

This could not be happening. How could something this integral to who she was be hidden her entire life?

"You said your biological father wasn't who raised you," Aurora said. "Did your mother ever say anything about him?"

"She might not have known he was a witch, depending on the circumstances," Lilly added.

"My mother died when I was five."

"I'm so sorry." To her credit, Aurora looked it. "But that could have contributed to you not knowing you were a witch. Your mother might have been waiting to tell you."

"I don't think so." Gia's mother couldn't have known, could she?

Lilly raised her hands like she was trying not to spook a wild animal. "We don't know your family, and aren't trying to rewrite anything. But you possess magical power, and we can teach you to use it if you want."

Gia collapsed onto the couch. *Use magic?* She could learn to cast spells? Lilly had said wards were protective. Could she use her magic to keep herself safe? To keep the Balzanos away?

Absurdly, the idea made Gia want to punch a hole in the wall. She'd had this power the whole time and not known. Her life could have been so different.

Regret and longing for what could have been threatened to crush her, clawing at her insides and shredding her heart. But Gia could still have a better life. Even if she wished she'd discovered magic a decade ago. Now was better than never.

Maybe she had the power to stop her father's growing empire after all. Maybe...

Ice formed in her veins. "Could not knowing I have magic make me sick?"

What if her headaches were her magic? What if having power and not using it was what was wrong with her brain? It would explain why every doctor was so baffled by her condition.

Aurora perched beside her on the couch, her form flickering as concern lined her face. "What do you mean, sick?"

Gia's insides twisted, but there was no point keeping it to herself now. "I get headaches. Really bad migraines, and I black out. I lose time and can't remember anything after the pain sets in."

"Your magic wouldn't do that to you," Aurora said, her voice firm.

But how could she know? "What if the headaches are my magic trying to escape?"

"Magic doesn't do anything unless you actively ask it to," Lilly said again. "I've never heard of a witch experiencing adverse effects because they possessed magical power they didn't use."

Gia's heart sank. Having an answer would have been such a fucking relief. "Could the headaches and memory loss be a spell someone cast on me?" That made even more sense. No wonder medical professionals couldn't help her.

Aurora and Lilly shared a look.

Lilly shook her head, seeming uneasy for the first time. "Unless someone was there, casting a spell on you every time you got a headache, it can't be a spell, and witches can't alter memories, period. Our power can do a great many things, but we can't craft illusions strong enough to result in memory loss."

"How do you know someone didn't cast a spell on me once, when I was ten, rather than every time I get a headache? It could have been causing my headaches ever since. Memory loss could be my body's response to pain rather than directly caused by the magic."

Lilly crossed her arms, her features twitching with alarm. "I can check if any curses or spells are lingering on you. But it's highly unlikely someone could have cast a spell that lasted from your childhood until now. The amount of power they would have needed..."

"Well, it can't be someone casting spells every time I get a headache." Gia was alone when the headaches hit often enough. These days, her family was never far, but she'd had headaches in the middle of class before. Unless... "Could someone cast a spell on me if they weren't with me?"

"Giving physical symptoms from afar is complex and difficult to pull off," Aurora said. "But we can check you to be sure."

Lilly nodded. "Give me some of your blood, and I can examine it. Any spells cast on you in the last few weeks will register. Have you had a headache recently?"

She hadn't had a blackout since running from her family. Her heart skipped, but it was probably a coincidence. She'd gone weeks without a migraine before. "The last one was nearly two weeks ago."

"It should still register."

Gia ran a hand through her hair. She hadn't missed the part where Lilly said she needed blood, but she had to know. If this was what had been wrong all these years... "Tell me what to do."

All Lilly needed was a tiny amount of blood. Gia pricked her finger and let a few droplets fall into a bowl, then watched as Lilly muttered, waving her hands over the blood. Aurora sat so still, she might as well have been frozen.

After a few minutes, Lilly met Gia's stare. "I can't detect any spells."

"You're sure?"

She nodded.

Gia fought her disappointment.

Aurora frowned. "Isn't this a good thing? It means no one in your life was lying to you and hurting you behind your back."

Except her family had lied and hurt her all the time, right to her face, just not physically. "You're right," Gia said, not wanting to get into it. "I can't see anyone in my life having magic anyway."

Franco Balzano didn't need magic. He had enough power already, wielding fear like a weapon.

Imagine how much worse it could have been.

Lilly scooped up the bowl and stood. "You can go to an apothecary if you're after herbs to help with your headaches. Even though magic wasn't the answer, it can still help."

Gia almost said no, then caught herself. "Maybe. Magic is about the only thing I haven't tried."

TWELVE

AURORA

CHECKING GIA for curses wasn't the direction Aurora had thought Lilly's visit would take. She'd love to peek into Gia's mind, see how she'd gone from denying magic had anything to do with her, to thinking magic had been harming her for years.

Maybe it wasn't anything more than distrust of the unknown, assuming magic must be responsible for all that was wrong and unexplained in her life. Aurora would admit, up until now, she'd been too wrapped up in her own problems to focus on anything else. With Lilly here, Aurora wasn't consumed by helplessness and could take a step back to consider Gia more thoroughly.

Was Gia's distrustful nature all about magic and the shock of finding out ghosts and witches were real? Aurora couldn't shake the feeling that there was more to it.

Lilly took her time casting a ward over the condo to stop Trey from entering, at least without breaking the spell and alerting Lilly.

"There," she said when the spell was finished. "That'll be better than nothing, but you can't stay cooped up here for long. What's the plan?"

If only Aurora had one. "As much as I want to storm into the Thornfield compound and find my body, I need to know if Trey's found me or if he's after the Lockwoods."

"He must have found you," Lilly said, taking a look out the window to confirm he hadn't left. "If Trey knows your soul is here, he may have followed Gia after sensing her magic. To check if she was heading out to find your body or help you in some way."

Electric ice rippled through Aurora. "I hadn't thought of that."

"Of course not. You didn't know I had magic," Gia said from where she was curled into the corner of the couch.

Aurora had been pretty sure Gia possessed magic even if she hadn't confirmed it, but she didn't argue the point. Guilt for bringing this on her threatened to overshadow everything else. She faced Lilly. "If that's the case, what's Trey waiting around for? Why not break in and come after me?"

"He might not know how to capture you, and is keeping an eye in the meantime. Or perhaps he wants a better idea of what he's up against. He doesn't know who else is here with you, and if he knows Lockwood headquarters is across the street, he might think we're all here."

"Are coven headquarters listed in the witch registry?" Gia asked, tone dry.

Despite her growing unease, Aurora snorted in amusement. Gia's lips twitched, and Aurora felt lighter. "There's no registry."

"You never know." Gia shrugged. "So, how'd he find out where your headquarters are?"

"The Lockwoods' association with the theater isn't a secret in the magic community," Lilly said, pausing at the door. "Which is why he could theoretically have a purpose for lurking other than Aurora. I'll update everyone on what's happening on the off chance Trey is scoping us out while we're between leaders."

"I don't want to say that would be ideal. It's not, but…" Aurora deflated. She didn't want the Thornfields to have their sights set on the Lockwoods. Not at all. Nothing good would come of it. But selfishly, it scared her less than her coven working out where she was and how to recapture her.

"I know," Lilly said, full of understanding. "It would make retrieving your body easier, but it feels unlikely. I can't imagine what the Thornfields would want with us."

Aurora couldn't either.

Gia's brow pinched, studying Aurora. "So you're saying, best-case scenario, your family thinks you…died?"

She nodded. Gia looked horrified, and there was something wrong with Aurora because Gia's concern made her skin prickle.

Lilly opened the condo door, oblivious to Aurora's ridiculous feelings. "I'll let you know what I find out, but don't expect to be sitting in ideal territory. Getting your body back will probably mean facing the Thornfields head on. We'll need to be ready." She gave an apologetic smile as she said goodbye and left.

The door clicked shut, and silence fell over the room. Gia probably needed space to process everything she'd learned, but it wasn't like Aurora could go far. She also didn't want to leave. Chasing that comforting prickling sensation was much more appealing than dwelling on the jam she'd gotten herself into.

Gia stared into the middle distance, clearly a thousand miles away, so Aurora banished her desire for closeness and drifted over to the window to watch Trey. He didn't follow Lilly as she strode down the street and disappeared from sight.

If he'd followed Gia because she was a witch, why not do the same now?

"Is my magic keeping you here?" Gia asked abruptly.

Spinning around, Aurora eyed her, but her expression didn't give anything away. "No. Like Lilly said, your magic can't do anything without your direct guidance. You're not casting a spell to trap me, are you?"

Gia stiffened, a scowl creasing her soft face. "Of course not. As long as you're sure it can't be subconscious."

"One hundred percent sure. I'm probably tied to you for the same reason I was tied to the theater: my growing link to the Lockwoods."

Gia chewed her bottom lip. "So I'm in the Lockwood Coven then? Because I'm related to Susan by blood?"

Aurora drifted closer. "You can be in the coven, if you want. There's a potential link, or the beginning of a link forming. But you don't have to join if you don't wish to. It's not like my family, where you're trapped from birth."

"Good. As long as they aren't going to force the issue."

"Most covens would never. My family is just particularly fucked up. Really, if you'd found out about magic from anyone other than me, I bet you wouldn't be worried."

Gia's lips parted, her expression giving the impression she disagreed. "What's Trey up to?"

That wasn't what Aurora expected her to say. "Looking at his phone."

"Is he going to be there all evening? I'd have bought more food if I'd known I couldn't leave again."

"Get delivery," Aurora suggested absently, not taking her eyes off Trey.

This might not be as bad as the windowless room in the theater, and nowhere near as bad as the Thornfield compound, but being confined grated like nettle on tender skin. And now Gia was trapped too. Involving someone unsuspecting was bad enough, but Aurora had to go and be selfish about it. Gia was the kind of woman who'd have caught her attention regardless of the situation, and Aurora couldn't deny that part of her was relieved they were stuck together.

It was almost as if whatever had drawn Aurora's soul to Gia knew her heart's desire and had given it to her. She didn't know Gia, but what she'd seen had her craving more. Each snarky remark, her determination, her beauty—it all captivated Aurora.

Maybe her feelings were heightened in this form. Maybe it was harder to hide from her inner self when her essence ruled her. Whatever it was, Aurora didn't want to leave her, no matter how horrible this situation was, and Gia deserved better than that.

Gia busied herself ordering pizza over the phone, and Aurora tried to pretend everything was normal. She was hanging out with a friend, not complicating Gia's life. Then Gia said, "It feels weird not getting you anything. You won't starve, right?"

A chill rippled through Aurora. "I shouldn't. My body is preserved by magic."

"Like Sleeping Beauty?"

Aurora snorted, the cold feeling vanishing. "I guess. But it'd be pretty fucked up if anyone tries to kiss me."

Gia's lip curled. "Gross."

"I assume you mean kissing an unconscious person, not kissing *me*."

"Obviously." Gia rolled her eyes.

Aurora's heart fluttered, or, near where her heart would be if she had a body, a light tingly sensation erupted, an image of Gia kissing her filling her mind.

Would Gia be down for some conscious, consensual kissing? There was no real point in asking at present, but when Aurora had actual lips again, she should bring it up. If Gia didn't run the moment they were unbound.

Aurora glanced back at Trey, her mood souring. The man still wasn't doing more than loitering.

There was a rustling sound, and Aurora turned. Gia was digging her hand into a cereal box, the inner bag discarded on the counter. She pulled out a stack of cash.

"Holy shit," Aurora said before she could stop herself.

Gia froze. "What? Is it Trey?"

"No." Aurora pointed. "How much money is that?"

Gia's cheeks bloomed with color. "It's nothing."

"Are those ones? Do you strip?"

Her cheeks got even redder. "No! I don't strip. They're twenties."

"Meaning that stack of cash isn't *nothing*."

Gia peeled a few bills free and shoved the rest back into the box. "I don't have a bank account right now."

Like *that* wasn't suspicious.

Aurora schooled her expression. Gia wouldn't open up if she felt judged, and Aurora wasn't judging. She was just shocked. "Do you get paid in cash?"

Gia shoved the unopened bag of cereal into the box. "I don't have a job right now. This is my savings."

"Okay." Aurora wasn't sure it was the truth. Gia seemed closed off, guarded in a way she hadn't been when talking about anything else, even her headaches. "Sorry, I didn't mean to pry."

Gia arched a brow.

"I only meant to pry a little," Aurora amended. "It's not every day I see that much money. No shade if you sell weed or whatever."

"I do not sell weed or strip. And yeah, no judgment to anyone who does, but I'm unemployed," Gia said, calmer than before.

Aurora didn't buy her nonchalance. "You're the only unemployed person I know with stacks of twenties lying around."

Gia lifted her chin, her composure fully in place now. "Maybe I robbed a bank."

Aurora snorted. They could pretend this wasn't a strange development all they wanted, but what the fuck? There was a hell of a lot more to Gia than Aurora had thought, and it had nothing to do with magic.

Damnation, nothing drew Aurora in like a mystery. Secrets. A little danger. She wanted to be the keeper of all Gia's hidden pieces. Her protector, her co-conspirator, pulling answers into the light.

Most of all, Aurora wanted to earn Gia's trust.

She drifted closer. "Seriously, whatever's up with—" She gestured toward the cereal. "You can tell me. You won't shock me. I'm literally a ghost."

Gia didn't crack. If anything, she closed off further. "It's nothing. I found out I inherited this place and decided to move, taking what I had with me. I don't trust banks, okay? Who knows what they do with your money."

"Okay." Aurora didn't believe her, but pushing wasn't working, so she resolved to drop it.

A buzzer sounded, and Gia jumped, her careful composure shattering as a hand flew to her chest, gripping her hoodie.

Yeah, she was hiding something important. Maybe even dangerous.

"Pizza's here." Gia hurried over to the intercom and buzzed the delivery person in.

Aurora checked out the window, and sure enough, Trey wasn't paying the pizza delivery any attention.

Soon, the delivery was at the door. Gia paid the guy politely, and he thanked her with a grunt before turning to go.

"Hey, Gia," another voice called from the hallway.

Aurora willed herself invisible and zoomed over to see who it was.

"Hi, Viv." Gia jostled the pizza box, her other hand coming to rest on the door like she wanted to close it.

A petite, young woman with short black hair and a sleek all-black outfit grinned slyly at Gia. "Dinner smells good. How're you settling in?"

"Oh...fine." Gia glanced over her shoulder, right through Aurora toward the window.

"Don't worry, I won't keep you from a good pie. But I wanted to ask if you've noticed that guy handing around?"

"What guy?" Gia did an excellent job acting confused, as if she really had no idea Trey had been lurking across the street all day.

She was a good liar. Interesting.

"There's a man hanging around across the street. He's been there for hours, looking at the building," Viv explained.

"Oh. I hadn't noticed. Are you sure he isn't waiting for someone?"

"All day?"

"Right. No, that's weird." Gia sounded shocked. "Thanks for letting me know. I'll be careful, but I'm sure he'll leave."

"He better. If you need anything, I'm across the hall."

Aurora rolled her eyes at the eagerness in Viv's tone.

"Thanks. I'll see you around."

The door shut, and Aurora reappeared. "Who's she?"

Gia brought the pizza to the kitchen and grabbed a plate. "My neighbor."

"You two friends?"

"No." Gia looked confused—genuinely now—by the mere prospect. "Viv knocked on my door when I moved in, but I've been busy since. As you know."

Aurora bit back a grin. She had taken up an awful lot of Gia's time since they'd crossed paths. "Well, Viv seemed *friendly.*"

Gia took a slice of pizza to the couch. "Yeah. I wonder why." She took a bite, seeming to contemplate this new mystery.

Was she serious? Viv was probably excited to have a new neighbor closer to her age. Or she noticed that Gia was hot and wanted to get to *know* her. Aurora would, if she weren't busy being a damned ghost.

But Gia seemed suspicious of Viv, and it didn't seem like an act. Taken alongside the cash, Gia's attitude didn't come across as a casual antisocial reaction, shyness, or other form of social awkwardness. It pointed to something more sinister.

Who *was* Gia? Aurora wanted to know more than anything.

GIA LEFT an invisible Aurora watching Trey out the living room window and went to have a shower.

Would Aurora float there all night if Trey didn't leave? Gia hoped he'd go away, but then what would the two of them do if Aurora didn't have an excuse to stay by the window? Gia had a feeling the ghost wouldn't need sleep.

She stepped under the hot water, careful to keep her hair dry. What if Aurora had gotten bored looking out the window and followed her in here, invisible?

A thrill shot through Gia.

Clamping her eyes shut, she plunged her face into the shower spray and shook off the idea. Why had her mind gone there? Aurora wouldn't do something so invasive. But imagining Aurora watching as she stood here naked, her core tightened.

She bit her lip. Fucking hell, she was a creep. Of all damn things, *why* was she thinking about Aurora peeping on her? Magic was real—she possessed it—and here she was, spinning an inappropriate fantasy.

She didn't even know if Aurora was into women. With her

luck, Aurora wouldn't be. And if she was, there were better things to do than watch each other bathe.

Was it possible Aurora liked women? To find out for sure, Gia needed to ask. Which she would not be doing.

She'd posed that fateful question to Tessa the summer after high school. Years of crushing had Gia convinced that Tessa liked her as more than a friend—it wasn't just her, definitely not one-sided—and so she'd asked Tessa outright if she liked girls.

Gia's cheeks flamed, and it had nothing to do with the warm water. The shock on Tessa's face had been answer enough. It had given way to friendly confusion, as if Tessa thought Gia was messing around, and yet the most humiliating part had been how kind Tessa had been when she'd finally said no.

There was no one to blame for the discomfort but herself. Gia had gotten carried away, and while she was an adult now, prepared to actually talk to a woman about her feelings if she ever wanted to date one, the reality was just as terrifying.

It wasn't like Gia had gained more experience in college. She'd been confident in her identity as a lesbian, leaving any conflicted feelings firmly behind with her adolescence, but between her migraines and Salvator lurking around, her romantic life had been about as active as a graveyard.

Not that any of it mattered. She and Aurora were literally tied together, unable to separate. Bringing up feelings and attraction was the dumbest idea. Nothing would summon awkwardness faster than Aurora saying she wasn't interested in women, or worse, saying she wasn't interested in Gia specifically.

No, thank you.

Inappropriate thoughts successfully squashed, Gia washed quickly and stepped out of the shower to dry off. The bathroom was attached to the bedroom, so she didn't have to traverse the living room in her towel. Thank god.

Gia pulled on a pair of pajama shorts and a T-shirt she'd been gifted with the rest of the clothes. Once dressed, she hovered, uncertain, in the empty bedroom. Now what? Leaving Aurora all alone, looking out the window all night, felt wrong.

Ugh, whatever. Gia was making this weirder than it needed to be.

She marched over to the door and yanked it open, calling out, "I'm going to sleep."

Aurora floated in the kitchen, not near the window at all. She gave a little start at Gia's words, disappearing, then reappearing a split second later. "Sounds good. Trey's gone, by the way."

"He is?"

"Yeah. He walked away not long after you went into the shower."

Because she was the most hopeless person on Earth, Gia's face heated. She rubbed the back of her neck, hoping Aurora didn't notice her flush at the mention of showering. "That's good, right?"

Aurora shrugged. "No one came to take over his post."

"Do you want to go out and..." Gia had no idea what they'd do. They'd established that going for Aurora's body could be dangerous if her coven were expecting them.

"Not unless you want to stock your fridge." Aurora's gaze swept over Gia, perhaps noting her sleeping attire.

She had to resist crossing her arms over her chest. "I'm not going anywhere tonight unless it's to help you."

Aurora smiled like Gia had said something really sweet, rather than betray how much of a homebody she was, not even wanting to go shopping after eight p.m. "I don't think there's much we can do tonight. Could you text Lilly with an update?"

"Sure." Gia ducked into the bedroom and grabbed her phone, glad to escape Aurora's gaze, even for a moment. She brought the phone to the doorway, not looking up as she typed. "I'm like a ghost secretary. Doing your bidding."

Jesus, why had she said *that?* There was nothing she wanted more than to do Aurora's bidding. She'd love for Aurora to tell her what to do...tell her what she needed.

Aurora huffed like she found Gia amusing. "Never thought I'd be important enough to have staff."

Gia's stomach dropped, and she forced a laugh, the sound strained. She'd had plenty of staff in Ashton Lakes, and it had nothing to do with being important, just being the daughter of a mob boss.

She cleared the lump forming in her throat. "Want me to tell Lilly anything else?"

Thankfully, Aurora seemed oblivious to her inner turmoil. "No, but make sure your phone stays charged so Lilly can get in touch. We'll need to know right away if anyone tampers with her ward."

"Yeah, I figured." Gia plugged the phone in, aware of Aurora drifting into the bedroom doorway behind her. "Do you sleep?"

Oh fuck, why had she asked? That sounded rude, didn't it? Or like she was about to invite Aurora in to sleep with her. She should be banned from talking.

"I can't," Aurora said smoothly, like she wasn't bothered. "Zoning out and losing track of time is as close as I get. I'll leave you in peace." She drifted into the living room.

Gia switched off the light and got into bed, pulling the covers over her. She immediately overheated and threw them off, rolling to her side.

Was Aurora going to zone out all night? It sounded dull as hell and far from restful.

She rolled over again. Dammit, she wasn't even tired. If

anything, her brain was kicking into gear now that everything had stopped.

She was a witch.

There was a ghost in her living room.

She had *magic powers*.

A random evil witch had followed her to the deli.

A gorgeous ghost was literally tied to her side.

Who knew how much time she had until Franco figured out she'd discovered her true parentage.

She had a crush on a ghost. After knowing her for *one day*, and believing she was a hallucination when they first met. What the fuck? Something was wrong with Gia, and it wasn't her migraines.

"Can't sleep?"

Gia yelped, sitting bolt upright.

Aurora floated in the doorway, glowing faintly, a hand on her hip. "I heard you tossing around."

Gia's cheeks flamed for no reason. "There's too much on my mind."

"Of course there is. You had a life-changing day."

Life-changing. Gia supposed that was true. For some reason, she'd expected Aurora to tell her to deal with it, like she would with anything else, or look at her like she was defective for not being able to suck it up.

Why had she expected Aurora to dismiss her like her father or brother would? She didn't seem like that kind of person.

"Do you want to talk about it?" Aurora asked.

Talk? God, no. Gia couldn't form words.

Aurora didn't let her hang for long, saying, "We could talk about something else."

Gia's stiff posture relaxed. "That might help."

Aurora floated closer, her ghostly form positively sparkling in the dark. "Is it okay if I sit? Hovering over you feels kind of creepy."

Gia's heart hammered as she straightened the tangled blankets. "Sure." She scooted over, even though there was already plenty of room.

Be cool.

Her heart did not calm down in the slightest as she lay back, eyes on the ceiling. Light from the street filtered through a gap in the curtains, casting a low glow across the white plaster, its luminescence flat compared to Aurora's dynamic glow. How odd for a person to cast light instead of shadow.

Not being alone or in her Ashton Lakes room was odd in itself. Gia was used to the trees surrounding the Balzano estate, their shadows dancing on the walls. Used to the silence of feeling cut off from the world by the sprawling grounds. Used to the loneliness of having no one to talk to, even in a house full of people.

Here, everything was different.

Aurora settled on the opposite side of the bed, brightening as she neared. Gia held her breath, afraid to give away her nerves. The mattress didn't dip under Aurora. There was no sound of rustling sheets, but Gia was more aware of her than she'd been of anyone in her entire life. This felt monumental, and Gia didn't know why.

For a moment, they both lay still as the dead, yet Gia felt more alive, more invigorated than she ever had.

"Is this what having a sleepover is like?" Aurora asked.

Gia cleared her throat. "Probably." *Other than the whole ghostly aspect, and the fact that this is somehow as life-changing as the rest of today.*

"Probably?" Aurora sounded surprised. "You didn't get to do sleepovers either?"

Gia caught herself just in time, almost admitting that daughters of big crime bosses weren't allowed to spend the night anywhere except in a fortified house. Gia cursed herself for nearly letting her guard down.

"I didn't really get invited to sleepovers when I was young." Which was mostly true. Kids whose families knew the Balzanos' reputation weren't inviting Gia anywhere unless their parents wanted in with Franco, and they weren't slumber party people. As for anyone oblivious to Gia's ties, RSVPing no a few times usually stopped the invites altogether. Once her migraines set in, she became known around school as someone who stayed home anyway.

"Me either," Aurora said. "I was homeschooled and didn't have many friends outside the coven until I was older. What about when you were older?"

Gia's heart skipped. Damn thing. "Like in college?"

"Yeah."

"I lived at home rather than in a dorm. Not exactly the classic experience, though I don't know if college sleepovers would have been like this." Oh my god, why had she said that? Now Aurora knew she had sex on the brain.

Except, lying here together, sex wasn't at the forefront of Gia's mind. This other kind of intimacy—to be close, to be trusted, to be gifted with secrets and dreams, and be free to give hers away in return—was something she'd craved even more fiercely than another woman's touch.

Maybe she didn't have to long for the intimacy of friendship anymore. Maybe she was in it right now.

Aurora chuckled. "You're right. I imagine college students weren't doing much sleeping. I didn't have a *classic* experience either. I didn't go to college."

Maybe that shouldn't have been a surprise. "Do witches often go to college?"

"Some do. Plenty of witches live semi-human lives and integrate into wider society, rather than spending every waking moment on a mission to serve Satan."

"You mean Satan as in the Devil?"

"He's not the Devil you know. Lucifer is just the immortal being who spread magic through humanity when he wasn't supposed to."

That didn't sound terrible, but there was probably more to it. "And how does your coven serve Satan? If he isn't evil, why is your coven so terrible?"

Aurora's glow flickered, but Gia didn't take her eyes off the ceiling, too afraid to break the spell of closeness. She liked Aurora sharing things with her.

"Serving Satan is mostly bullshit, and doesn't have much to do with him," Aurora admitted. "Lucifer is to thank for our magic, but most witches don't obsess over him as a figurehead. He made no decrees and gave no guidance for who witches should be."

"Doesn't sound like much of a leader."

"He isn't. Not to witches, at least. Demons are probably another story. Witches, like my coven, use 'serving Satan' as an excuse to act however they want, pretending it serves a greater purpose. Suffering proves we're worthy of the gifts bestowed on us. If you're a lower member of the coven, that is. Leaders and their advisors are above all that. They make you suffer."

Fucking hell. She said it so nonchalantly, like suffering was normal. Gia supposed in a way, it was. Removing the Satan of it all, the set-up Aurora described wasn't altogether unfamiliar.

Gia swallowed, not sure if she should, but asked anyway, "And the marriage thing?"

Aurora flickered once more, but she didn't seem to hesitate as she answered. "Covens like mine are all about forming alliances. Building power. The Thornfields have been trying to expand their territory for years. We don't have power in the city and are stuck on the outskirts, so my uncle looked farther afield, and finally picked a coven from the Rocky Mountains to join forces with."

"That's far." Not even Gia's father had tried to expand that broadly, as far as she knew.

"You have to cast a wide net," Aurora said bitterly. "Most witches aren't like the Thornfields or Nightingales. There were probably closer covens interested in an alliance to increase their territory, but my uncle wants more than territory. He wants witches like him. Cruel people looking to manipulate others into serving them."

"Is that why Trey might be scoping out the Lockwoods? To see if they'll serve your coven?" She chanced a glance at Aurora, who was staring hard at the ceiling.

"The Lockwoods would be a bad coven to overtake. You need to go after witches who share enough of your beliefs that you can ensnare them. The Lockwoods would resist getting involved at all, or die trying."

"Damn."

Aurora glanced over, a guilty look on her face. "Everything I said probably sounds really fucked up. Sorry."

"Don't be. Your coven is the one terrorizing people to the point they'd rather die. They're the fucked-up ones who should be sorry."

There was a long pause, and Gia had no clue what more to say. Her chest swelled with the ease with which Aurora opened up. She wished she could reciprocate, but she'd never fought against the evil she'd grown up with. What would she even say?

"The Nightingales aren't people my uncle can manipulate," Aurora said after a while. "He sees their leader, Arthur, as an equal, and Arthur has some business in Shearwater Landing that Uncle Stan wants to help with. Maybe he thinks he can gain power within the city that way."

"Is Arthur who you were supposed to marry?"

"Fuck no. Though his son won't be any better. I've never met Harper, but Arthur is rotten, the kind of person who takes pride in molding their offspring into horrible, mini versions of themselves. Even the way he smiles is slippery and gross. It's no wonder he's big into blood magic."

Gia was afraid to ask what she meant, but Aurora wasn't done.

"My uncle is under no illusion I'd be a willing bride—he probably didn't tell the Nightingales—but they'd have figured it out quickly, and wouldn't have cared. They'd take my blood and use my power even if I didn't want to help them with their spells and schemes."

Gia's stomach dropped. "I'm sorry."

"Me too...and as bad as being trapped outside my body is, I'd rather this than what would have happened if I'd stayed. I don't regret taking the risk and fucking up. I'd do it again."

Gia rolled onto her side, chest pinching tight as a swell of determination surged through her. "We'll get your body. I promise. They won't win."

Their gazes locked, Aurora's eyes shimmering in the dark.

Gia had never done anything about her family, but she could do something to help Aurora, and she wouldn't stop trying until they succeeded.

"Thanks." Aurora extended a pale hand, resting her fingers on top of Gia's.

A chill started in her hand and coursed through her body, a thousand tiny tingles lighting her up. Aurora's ghostly skin seemed to spark in response.

"You'll fit right in with the Lockwoods, you know. They're fierce like you."

"I'm not fierce." But Gia could try to be. Do better than she had been.

Aurora pulled her hand away, a huff of misplaced disbelief filling the space between them. "You learned about magic *today* and promised to help me deal with an unprecedented magical situation. That's the definition of fierce."

A tendril of shame curled inside Gia. "Well, yeah. Of course I'll help. Sorry I was so resistant before."

"Because you didn't believe me? That's normal. Now that you know I'm in trouble, you offered to help. It's what any Lockwood would do. What family should do."

Family. Gia's heart ached. Her family never looked out for her. Sure, they protected her out of obligation, but the Balzanos never wanted what was best for her. For her to be happy and live the life she wanted. To help her reach her potential.

Longing for that kind of family nearly smothered Gia.

Aurora hadn't meant that the two of them were like family. She was talking about the Lockwood Coven, and even if Gia wasn't as wary of her aunt's coven as she'd been, she didn't belong with them.

THEIR CONVERSATION DRIFTED AWAY from heavier topics and slowed to a crawl. Aurora watched Gia slip into sleep, transfixed by her unguarded expression. Those soft cheeks and pouting lips. Gia's utter relaxation made Aurora acutely aware of how poised she'd been in every waking moment, even when Aurora had thought she'd glimpsed cracks in her veneer.

It seemed Gia was always on her guard. She hadn't shared much as they'd talked.

Why had she lived at home during college? She'd hardly said anything about her family, and hadn't talked about them in relation to her move to Shearwater Landing. Not the way someone with a strong familial connection would, so it didn't seem like she'd lived at home out of a loving desire to stay close.

Aurora let her curiosity go. She'd have to be patient if she wanted to get to know Gia. She wouldn't spill her life story in a day, even if Aurora had no qualms about answering any question she threw at her, giving as much of herself as Gia asked for.

Would Gia be pleased Aurora was lying here, watching her sleep, admiring the faint freckles on her cheeks? Aurora tried not to be creepy about it, but she couldn't pry herself away.

Being near Gia felt right. Centering, no *grounding*. Her soul longed to close the distance between them, an electric force tugging them together.

Was this feeling nothing more than the magic tying them together, akin to whatever had called her to the theater? Aurora wanted to say no. She hadn't felt like this trapped in the office. This pull felt like it came from within. It was stronger now than it had been earlier, as if it were growing along with her personal connection to Gia.

That, or Aurora's mind was running away with itself, lost in an abundance of time and lack of sleep, leading her to fantasy.

Sometime after the sun had risen, Gia stirred and rolled onto her back. The moment she shifted into consciousness, Aurora swore a zap of energy ignited in the still morning air, calling her soul to attention.

"Hey." Gia's soft voice was heavy with sleep as she turned to look at her.

"Morning," Aurora said in a low rasp, the charge between them heightening.

Gia shifted, seemingly oblivious to the spark. She stretched, the blanket falling away, and settled closer to Aurora, a tiny smile shaping her lips. Her lashes fluttered, and Aurora longed to obliterate the distance separating them.

Gia stilled, her attention settling on Aurora. Were her feelings written all over her face? If they were, Gia didn't look displeased. Her cheeks flushed, and Aurora didn't think it was the warmth of the bed.

Gia had to feel this connection too, didn't she?

Can I kiss you? The words were on the tip of Aurora's tongue. Except she couldn't kiss Gia. Not really.

She'd touched Gia's hand last night, but it had been a struggle not to pass through her to the mattress below. Why was touching Gia different than touching a wall or lying on the bed?

Why didn't Gia's body contain Aurora like any other physical object?

Gia's lips parted. Fuck it. They could still kiss, in their own way. Aurora could at least ask—

The shrill beeping of Gia's phone cut through the air.

Gia jumped, giving a tiny yelp. "Shit. That scared me." She shot a sheepish glance at Aurora.

"Same." But the crushing disappointment of a missed opportunity outweighed the small fright.

Gia sat up and grabbed her phone off the charger. "Oh my god, it's after ten. How did I sleep so late?"

Aurora should have realized they'd spent most of the morning in bed. The sun was bright outside, but time hadn't seemed to exist before the phone went off, and not in the hopeless way it had when Aurora had been trapped in the theater.

"I got a text from Lilly," Gia continued, tapping the phone. "The Thornfields are saying..." A crease appeared on her brow.

Aurora floated into a sitting position. "What?"

"Sorry. The Thornfields have publicly announced your death. But Lilly can't tell if they genuinely believe it, or if they're covering up the truth and lying to people outside the coven. There's no indication that anyone is after the Lockwood Coven, so Trey's presence makes Lilly distrust what your family is saying."

"Dammit." Aurora wanted a simple answer, but Trey being here for the Lockwoods made less and less sense the more she thought about it, even if he had seemed interested in Gia. Something else occurred to her. "If my coven knows I'm suspending my body while my soul is elsewhere, and they're telling people I died, what are they going to do when I wake up?"

Gia glanced up, a grim expression stealing all the softness from her features. "It wouldn't matter if they don't plan on anyone outside the coven seeing you again."

Trapped even more thoroughly than before. Her coven could also be planning to kill her if she ever woke up, but she couldn't say that out loud. A stone dropped deep in Aurora's soul, threatening to drag her to the darkest depths.

"We won't let them cut you off from the world," Gia said, a hint of steel entering her tone. "And who knows? They could very well believe you died, and won't even notice when your body disappears from the crypt."

Aurora swallowed her dread, focusing instead on Gia's sweet determination. "Here's to hoping."

Gia flashed a reassuring smile. "Lilly said she's still looking into it. I'll reply with a thanks, unless you need me to add anything else?"

"No, all good. Thanks for checking."

Gia shrugged. "I don't mind being your ghost secretary."

Aurora grinned, grateful Gia could so effortlessly give her a reason to.

She set the phone aside. "Speaking of Trey, has he returned? Maybe we were all wrong about why he was here."

"Um." Aurora should have checked hours ago. "I'll go see." She quickly zoomed out of the room.

Fuck, she'd been completely distracted. They'd know if someone had messed with Lilly's protective ward, but Aurora needed to be proactive, not sit around watching Gia sleep like a weirdo.

She turned invisible and looked out the window, scanning the street. A few people were out and about, but no one she recognized, and none of them seemed to be lurking. No trace of Trey, either.

It was too much to hope that Trey and her coven had given up on whatever they'd been doing, or that they'd been completely wrong about why he was here, as Gia had suggested. Was the absence of loitering Thornfields a positive development or a brief reprieve while something worse brewed?

The sound of a sink running caught Aurora's attention.

A few minutes later, the water shut off, and Gia emerged from the bedroom, heading for the kitchen. "Is he there?"

Aurora let her invisibility drop. "No. And I don't see anyone else suspicious hanging around."

"That's a relief." Gia cut a slice of bread and popped it in the toaster.

"Maybe." Aurora only felt more certain that the absence was ominous. "We should head out and get anything you need. Maybe think about staying somewhere else."

Gia opened a jar of jam, lid popping. "Like where?"

"The Lockwoods will find room somewhere."

An all too familiar guarded expression settled over Gia's face. "I don't know. I mean, it's smart. I can't argue that." The unsaid *but* hung heavy in the air.

Aurora understood Gia's reluctance, but there wasn't time for her to slowly become comfortable with the Lockwoods. "I know you'd rather not stay with the coven. You can still decide to be involved with the Lockwoods, or not, after this is all over. They won't consider helping as a debt that needs repayment. I promise."

"Okay. I don't doubt they're as good as you say..." She trailed off. After a pause, she returned her attention to the toast.

So Gia trusted Aurora's word, but couldn't seem to extend that trust to the Lockwoods. Why? Was it because she didn't know enough of the coven personally, or was it something else? Something that couldn't be overcome.

Aurora didn't see Gia jumping into coven life any time soon, if ever, and with that realization, something else occurred to her. "What are you going to do with the theater?" Would she allow the coven to continue meeting there even if she didn't join? Aurora tried not to let that prospect disappoint her.

Gia grabbed a plate and a butter knife. "I'm going to sell the theater. This place, too."

"Sell it?" Aurora couldn't hide her shock.

"Yeah. Someone in the coven can buy it if they want. Actually, a private sale would be ideal. Quicker."

"Are you in a hurry?" Aurora couldn't help feeling blindsided. They hardly knew each other, and yet it hurt that Gia might not stick around.

Would Gia want to keep in touch when this mess was over? Aurora had taken it for granted that she did. She'd assumed Gia would want her to explain how to use magic at the very least.

Maybe the closeness Aurora experienced last night and this morning had been all in her head. Damnation. Good thing she hadn't asked for that kiss.

Gia shifted uncomfortably. "What do you mean, hurry? I was planning to sell the theater before I met you yesterday. I haven't had time to rethink it. That's all."

Aurora halted her sinking thoughts. There was no reason to freak out. Maybe Gia would reassess and change her mind. It wasn't as if she'd mentioned a life she was burning to return to. Aurora had the perfect chance to convince her to stay, tied together as they were.

"That's fair," she made herself say.

Gia nodded. "I should talk to the coven about the theater. Is it important to the Lockwoods? Beyond being headquarters, I mean."

"You could say that."

"Then I'll try my best to make sure it stays in their hands."

It was kind of her. Gia owed Aurora and the Lockwoods nothing.

Unfairly, Aurora wanted more.

The toast popped, and Gia spread jam on it. "We can figure out what's best for the theater while we hide out. I'll message Lilly about where to go, but if this takes too long to coordinate, someone could show up outside again, and we'll be stuck."

"Then let's go out now." Aurora glanced out the window. Still no one suspicious. "We can head to The Herb Emporium to see what we can do for your migraines while Lilly finds us a place to stay."

Gia carefully chewed a bite of toast, almost like she was buying herself time. "You think the apothecary is worth a try?"

"Sure. The guy who runs The Herb Emporium is a friend of the coven. Seems like a decent witch from everything I've heard. You could even bring your pills to show what you've tried."

Gia frowned. "Is an apothecary like a magical pharmacist?"

"Sort of."

Gia considered as she finished her toast. She put the plate in the sink and grabbed the cereal box from the cupboard. "Okay. How much is this witch going to charge?"

THE COAST WAS STILL clear by the time they made it downstairs.

"I'll tell you if I spot anyone," Aurora whispered, floating invisibly at Gia's elbow.

There was a chance someone was hiding in a stealthier location than Trey had been, but they'd have to be within sight of the building's entrance or both ends of the street to tail Gia.

As Gia stepped outside, Aurora had a thorough look around, spotting no one. Had they read the situation all wrong? She couldn't imagine how. But then, what was she missing?

The answer might lie with Gia rather than the Lockwoods

or Thornfields. She was cagey and had a suspicious stack of cash she refused to explain. But how could money lead to Trey? The Thornfields didn't deal with humans, and Gia's shocked reaction to magic couldn't have been fake.

Aurora would bet her soul on it.

At least no one Aurora recognized popped out of the woodwork to follow them. She'd take the win and figure the rest out later.

The Herb Emporium wasn't far, and Gia had the address and a map pulled up on her phone, saving Aurora from whispering directions in her ear.

Reaching the end of the block, Gia turned down a cross street. An SUV pulled into traffic behind them, and Gia looked over her shoulder. She wore dark sunglasses, her expression unwavering, but the glance alone was enough to have Aurora on alert.

"I don't recognize the vehicle," Aurora said, confident it didn't belong to her coven. They were more of a pickup truck crew.

"Good." Gia strode forward with apparent confidence, her hands fisting around her backpack straps.

Was that a hint of nerves?

Trey or someone else could be in a car Aurora didn't know—they might have rented one—but after yesterday's obvious stakeout, stealth didn't fit. Still, Aurora floated into the street to get a better look. Two unfamiliar men were visible through the front windshield. She drifted out of the way, and the SUV overtook Gia, stopping at the next intersection.

Another car pulled out and followed suit. It was all normal traffic. Nothing to worry about. They were being paranoid, even if for good reason.

No one seemed to follow them as Gia walked several more blocks. The SUV and following car both veered off course before Gia made her next turn. Of course, there were more similar SUVs around, which wasn't unusual.

Aurora did her best to look into as many vehicles as she could, and didn't see anyone she recognized.

They paused at a red light. Maybe after the apothecary, they could go to a coffee shop to wait until Lilly coordinated a safe place for them. A relaxing environment would do them both good, even if Aurora had to stay hidden.

With a screeching of tires, a black SUV rounded the corner, going way too fast. Gia swore in surprise, and Aurora flinched. The vehicle came to an abrupt halt, blocking the crosswalk in front of them.

Gia stiffened and staggered back. It was a good thing she hadn't been stepping off the curb to cross on the red light, or she'd have been hit. *Shit*, Aurora fumed. Gia could have died!

Assholes. Traffic wasn't even holding them up. Why stop?

The rear door to the SUV swung open, and a middle-aged man in a leather jacket with slicked back hair jumped out.

Gia gasped, taking two quick steps away from him.

"There you are," he said roughly. "I think you need to come with me."

What the fuck?

"And before you run"—the man opened his jacket, revealing a shoulder holster and a fucking *gun*—"think about what you're doing. You don't want anyone to get hurt, do you?"

"*Salvator*." Gia's back was stiff as a board. Aurora could hear her heart thundering, could practically feel the frantic vibrations through the air, rattling her soul.

Gia knew this guy?

"Get in the car," he ordered, tone threatening.

Gia looked wildly around. "I can't."

"You don't have to," Aurora said in her ear. But fuck, what could she do? She couldn't cast a single damn spell in this form.

"*Now*," the man—Salvator—snapped, reaching beneath his jacket.

Gia whimpered, taking a reluctant step forward.

Like hell. Aurora wouldn't let her go with him. Gia may have left out a mountain's worth of details when telling Aurora about herself, but that didn't matter in the slightest. She was in trouble.

Gia took another step closer. A horn blared. The SUV was blocking traffic, but Salvator had the air of someone who didn't give a fuck, his arm tucked under his jacket like he was holding the gun, ready to draw it any second.

Fury burned through Aurora. She was so damn sick of men like him. She didn't need to know Salvator to know his type. And she wasn't letting him get his paws on Gia.

Aurora zoomed in front of Gia, her will to be invisible evaporating, replaced with the consuming desire to be seen. To take up space and scare the shit out of this fucking guy.

Energy crackled, and Gia gasped, halting her steps before they collided. Aurora raised her arms, translucent skin glowing. "Leave," she growled, dropping her voice low.

"*Merda!*" Salvator's eyes went wide, and in one swift motion, he drew his gun.

Oh, Satan. That wasn't supposed to happen.

Salvator's surprise quickly faded into cold determination. He pointed the gun through Aurora's translucent form, right at Gia. "In the goddamn car, Gianna. Now."

Seriously? He wasn't shitting himself when faced with a real-life ghost? Who the hell was this guy?

Aurora had to do something, except yet again, she was helpless. A witch who couldn't use her magic to do what truly mattered: protect herself and the people she cared for.

"Okay," Gia said, like it pained her, before stepping forward. *Through* Aurora.

Electric chills enveloped Aurora's entire being, and she gasped. Gia gasped too, as if they were one, and Aurora swore she felt air in her phantom lungs.

Gia's fear crashed into her. Aurora sensed her hopelessness, her regret, all as if they were her own emotions. She felt Gia's pounding heart, but not in the electric way she had before. Blood pulsed through Aurora, flowing stronger than it ever had in her own body.

Gia shuddered, and Aurora's soul shook, a shared cold dread threatening to smother them both.

Satan. Aurora was inside Gia, joined together in a way she hadn't thought possible. And here, in the depths of Gia's being, swirling along with her despair and fear, was her magic, bright and bursting to be used.

Aurora seized it as she would her own, and when she spoke, Gia's mouth moved.

"Run," they said, voice a booming echo.

Salvator's mouth dropped open. He blinked, grip tightening on his handgun. "Stop fucking around and get in the car, or I'll shoot every single person on this street."

Aurora raised her hand, Gia's hand, and for the first time, her power wasn't restricted when she needed it most. She could fight back. Aurora muttered a spell, slashing her hand upward, and Salvator was thrown into the side of the SUV, hard.

He grunted, slumping to the side, and she took a step forward. Gia's power sang in her grasp, seeming to grow, opening up to reveal a well far greater than anything Aurora had ever found within herself.

Damnation, Gia was powerful.

Excitement sparked within Aurora's soul, lighting up Gia's body as unexpected joy filled them. Aurora tipped her head back and laughed.

Salvator scrambled to his feet, waving his gun, all composure gone. "What the fuck!"

Aurora hit him with another wave of power, and he grabbed the hood of the SUV to steady himself. She poured magic into the metal, heating it to scorching in an instant.

Salvator screamed, nearly dropping the gun in his other hand. He clutched his burnt hand to his chest and ducked into the back seat. "Drive!"

The SUV's tires screeched, and it peeled out from the curb, tearing down the street, the path ahead clear.

The rest of the intersection cleared slowly. People on the other side of the street stared, but they wouldn't have seen exactly what happened behind the SUV, and no one was on the sidewalk behind them.

"We have to go," Gia's rough voice vibrated through Aurora, her throat tingling. "Before the cops are called."

Gia didn't wait for a reply, quickly returning the way they'd come and ignoring the concerned questions volleyed at her as people rushed over.

Aurora should leave, float beside Gia as she had been before, but the idea of separating felt akin to hurting herself. She couldn't.

"Don't go," Gia choked out. "Stay there. Please."

It was like she'd read Aurora's thoughts. Could she? Aurora couldn't hear Gia's, but there wasn't much difference between mind-reading and sharing their most intimate emotions.

Gia was like an open book, yearning for connection with a ferociousness that rocked Aurora to her core.

She wouldn't leave. She'd stay forever if Gia asked.

FIFTEEN

GIA

Gia's heart beat frantically as she hurried down the street, hardly able to concentrate on where she was going. Wind rushed in her ears, or was it her blood pounding? Her whole body tingled, bright and electric. She wanted to squirm out of her skin and fall into the sensation all at once.

Aurora was *inside* her. Possessing her? No, Gia still had control. But Aurora had...she had used Gia's magic.

Gia had felt her magic for the first time as it burst from her, following Aurora's expert guidance. Seeing Salvator fly backward, completely helpless, had been a rush like no other. Gia needed more. She needed to learn to harness her power. Think what she could do then. She could face Franco. Punish him for his crimes and get justice for her mother, and that was only the beginning of what she could accomplish.

The feeling of magic was addictive. So bright, Gia was breathless. Would it be the same without Aurora? As exhilarating? How much of this flying-high feeling was Aurora rather than the power itself?

Gia's longing to be close to Aurora flared, a tangle of desire winding through her. Gia's face flamed. Fuck. Could Aurora sense the sexual nature of her feelings? The root of her longing for closeness? Was she giving herself away?

She'd sensed Aurora's determination when they'd joined. Her rage. Aurora must feel Gia's desire in the same way.

Before mortification could solidify, something soothing flared in response to Gia's desperation, hot and possessive. Carnal.

Oh.

Gia scrambled to open the door to her building and ran up the stairs.

"Gia," Viv called as they passed each other on the second-floor landing, Viv heading downward.

Gia ignored the woman, hurrying by without stopping. Even speaking was too much right now. Concentrating on anything other than Aurora was impossible.

Gia reached her condo and unlocked the door. "Oh my god," she gasped, throwing the door closed behind her.

Sweat prickled her skin, her body hot as shivers cascaded down her spine, settling in her core. "Holy fucking shit." Her head dropped against the door, the urge to shove her hand into her jeans and chase her release nearly over-whelming.

With a moan on her lips, Gia's body trembled. Suddenly, Aurora appeared in front of her, glowing brighter than Gia had ever seen.

The intense urge to give in to the ache growing between her thighs faded. *Oh no.* What had she almost done? What if she'd gotten confused and that carnal desire had been all hers, not Aurora's?

Gia's face burned.

But Aurora's stare was molten, not angry. "I should have asked to kiss you this morning after all."

"W-what?" Gia sagged against the door.

Aurora's gaze dragged down Gia's body, then up again, landing on her lips. "I should have asked to kiss you."

Gia swallowed. "You're attracted to me?"

Fuck, she sounded like an idiot, but she had to be sure. More than sure. This felt like a fantasy. Gia hardly believed it was happening for real.

Aurora cocked her head, curious rather than mocking. "Can't you feel it?"

"I wasn't sure if it was all me..." But her arousal had dimmed when they'd disconnected, like Aurora had taken hers with her.

Aurora floated closer until they were almost touching. "It wasn't all you. I want to be close to you, Gia. It's like you're calling to me. You intrigue me. And I want to make you feel good."

Gia bit her lip. She wanted that too. She wanted to ignore her fear. Ignore what happened in the street and what it meant, and have this one good thing. "I'd have said yes if you'd asked."

Aurora hummed a soft, satisfied sound. "How about now?"

"Please." Gia meant to say yes, not betray her utter desperation. Then again, Aurora had already felt it firsthand. What was the point in hiding?

Aurora leaned in, and Gia's eyes fell shut. A sensation almost like a tiny breeze ghosted her skin, tingles overwhelming her lips and spreading along her cheeks. The sensation faded, and Gia opened her eyes to find Aurora pulling away.

She chased Aurora's pale lips, crashing their mouths together and meeting no resistance.

Waves of chills and sparks danced across her face. This wasn't at all how Gia imagined her first kiss. It was better. The sensation of Aurora's mouth on her drew her in. Their bodies pressed together, but instead of physical pressure, there was awareness, a kind of openness to more.

Electricity sparked in Gia's chest, radiating to her core. Her thigh muscles tensed, the ache between her legs as potent as it'd been when Aurora was inside her.

"Aurora," Gia moaned, longing to wrap her arms around the ghost, to hold this open feeling tight and not let it go.

"Does that feel good, baby?" Aurora cooed, brushing glowing fingers along Gia's neck.

She arched into it, head tipping to the side. "Yes."

Aurora's fingers trailed over Gia's lips, almost as electric as her kiss. "Where else do you like to be touched?"

Gia's inexperience raised its ugly head, and uncertainty threatened to extinguish her arousal.

"What's wrong?" Aurora asked immediately, her hand falling away.

"Who said anything was wrong?"

"You seized up. If this is too weird...or not what you want..."

"It's not that." Gia searched for the words. She hated having to say anything and wished everything could happen the way she wanted, but she needed Aurora too much to let the chance slip away. Especially for a reason as silly as not being able to speak her mind. "I don't want to tell you what to do."

Aurora's smile gleamed. "You want me in charge?"

Gia nodded.

"What if I asked you to show me how you get yourself off?"

Gia froze again. She tried not to, but fuck. "Um."

"Not into that? No problem."

"Are you?"

Aurora's cheeks glowed brighter. "I'd love to watch you get lost in yourself. See you relax and let loose. You'd be gorgeous."

"I could try."

A furrow appeared between Aurora's brows. "Only if it excites you. You don't have to do it just for me. Not if you prefer something else."

Dammit. She was going to have to admit it. "I don't have

enough experience to have preferences. All I know is I want you. Any way you want to touch me. I just...need you."

Aurora's hungry gaze softened, not losing any of its heat as understanding dawned. "I've got you." She threaded a hand through Gia's hair, the other stroking her arm.

A giddiness bubbled inside Gia's chest. "You feel so good. So bright. Can you feel it?"

Aurora hummed. "Yeah, it's like a thousand tiny shocks when I touch you."

"Yes, like you're making my skin come alive."

Aurora moaned. "How about here?" Her hand moved along her collarbone.

"Yes." Gia pushed out her chest, unable to resist now that everything she'd longed for was dangling in front of her.

Aurora needed to touch her everywhere. Take her.

Their gazes locked, and Aurora brushed the swell of Gia's breast. Aurora traced with painful slowness, leaving Gia's bare skin to caress what was covered by her bra and shirt. The touch felt no different, the magic of their connection unhindered, the same way it had been when Aurora stepped inside her.

Gia might as well have been naked. She felt completely exposed, even though Aurora couldn't see through her clothes. Her breathing turned heavy, and at last, Aurora's fingers reached Gia's nipple, hard and as needy as the rest of her.

Gia moaned as Aurora circled the tight bud, shocks and vibrations zipping over her skin. Her core throbbed, wetness slicking her entrance, and she clenched her thighs, trying not to squirm.

"Do you need me to touch you lower?" Aurora teased.

"Please." Gia couldn't wait any longer. She wasn't even nervous. She'd always expected she would be, but didn't seem to have the brainpower.

Nothing mattered but Aurora's touch.

As she continued to tease Gia's nipple, Aurora's other hand traveled down her body. Gia instinctively reached for Aurora, trying to pull her closer, but her hands passed right through. How did this feel to Aurora? Gia needed to return her pleasure. She longed to feel the curves of Aurora's body. The softness of her skin. Every tingle was a treasure, but Gia needed Aurora in every way.

She palmed Aurora's breast as best she could. There was no swell of soft skin, no resistance, no give, nothing but cool shivers radiating up Gia's arm. But Aurora gasped, and Gia's heart sang at the look of ecstasy on her face.

"Do that again," Aurora begged as she did something unspeakable to Gia's nipple.

Gia touched Aurora, careful not to pass too far through her, skirting her edges like she was tracing something precious.

Cool electricity sparked between them, addictive against Gia's overheated skin. If only Aurora would fall forward. Consume her once more. But at the same time, this was too good to stop. Gia wanted it all at once. Aurora inside her. Aurora's hands on her. Her mouth. Her intense stare, boring into her. Her body beneath Gia's fingers.

Aurora's wandering hand reached Gia's mound and slipped effortlessly lower, tingles and sparks consuming Gia's labia, delving deeper and lighting her up from inside. Aurora found her clit, her touch right there without needing to spread her open.

Gia's spine arched, and she rolled her hips without thinking, her hands grasping for Aurora, diving past her breasts to her waist. "Aurora," she gasped, unable to look away from the fierce glow in her lover's eyes.

"You going to come for me, baby?" Aurora teased little circles around Gia's clit, the sensation overtaking her whole pelvic area, vibrating almost like a toy.

Gia's hips jerked, and everything pulled tight. Release pulsed through her, taking her by surprise and stealing her breath. Her inner walls clenched, and fuck if the sensation of Aurora's ghostly touch didn't pulse in response.

Aurora moaned, surging closer, pressing them together. She straddled either side of one of Gia's legs. Gia thrust, her orgasm cresting. Aurora shuddered and gasped, her glowing form flickering as a spark flared hot atop Gia's thigh.

Was that Aurora's orgasm? Renewed heat flared in Gia. Holy fucking shit. Aurora was gorgeous, her pale cheeks flushed and glowing, a hint of pink shining through. And her eyes, heavy-lidded but no less focused as she found her pleasure. Pleasure in Gia.

After a moment, Aurora dropped her head forward, a soft hum filling Gia's ear. Their noses brushed.

"You're like nothing I've ever felt," Aurora murmured against Gia's cheek.

She sagged, completely boneless. "So are you."

Sex with another solid body wouldn't be like this, but even if Aurora had her body, Gia couldn't imagine what they'd shared being different in the ways that counted. Not the sharp pull of Gia's desire. Or the way Aurora looked at her and touched her, confidently but carefully.

Potential seemed to unfurl before them, like this was the beginning of a connection more amazing than Gia had ever dreamed.

"That was wild." Aurora couldn't technically be breathless in this form, but the feeling of being unable to catch up consumed her all the same.

Gia's relaxed expression turned dreamy. "Wild... Electric."

"Yes, exactly. Electric." A tingling sensation slid along Aurora's spine, and she wanted nothing more than to cling to it. "As much as I'd love to strip you and do it all again..."

Gia's face fell, her thoughts no doubt following Aurora's.

Aurora pulled away ever so slightly. "Is it safe to stay here? What the hell happened? *Who* was that?"

Gia ducked around Aurora, avoiding her questioning gaze, and slid the backpack off her shoulders. The distance was jarring after being so close, but they couldn't act like they'd hurried home for nothing but a good time, no matter how much they both wanted to.

"I don't know if we're safe here," Gia admitted. "I...I'm going to go to the bathroom, and then we'll talk." She scurried away, disappearing into her room, the water in the bathroom running a moment later.

Fuck. Aurora was being a terrible lover. Especially if Gia

was inexperienced. But this was an extenuating circumstance. Endless orgasms, pampering, and lazy pillow talk were not what you did after someone attempted to abduct you at gunpoint.

Really, Aurora shouldn't have gotten so carried away. She never should have kissed Gia. But how could she not after experiencing Gia's arousal, her longing, her desire? Especially after the perfect way it had echoed and encouraged her own.

Gia had looked at Aurora like she'd held all the answers in the universe. It was irresistible.

Gia returned from the bathroom and checked out the window rather than join Aurora.

She drifted over, needing some physical closeness even if Gia didn't. "Who was that man?"

"Salvator. He works for my father."

Aurora floated a few inches higher, relieved that Gia wasn't playing coy. "And your father is...?"

Gia turned away from the window, her face blank and hopeless, devoid of all the beautiful life Aurora had seen moments ago. "Franco Balzano, head of the Ashton Lakes Italian mob."

All righty then. That was... Huh. "I guess mob ties explain the cash."

Gia's expression darkened. "You're right, I didn't earn a dime of that money."

"I didn't mean—"

"No, it's fine. I won't lie. I'm not..."

Aurora waited, but Gia didn't seem capable of bringing herself to say what she wasn't. Aurora tried again. "I'm guessing your father didn't approve of you coming here to claim Susan's inheritance?"

It was the wrong thing to say. Gia's dark expression twisted with worry. "I didn't tell him I was leaving. Susan's Lawyer, Edward Ramirez, and his friend Sam helped me escape."

"The Lockwoods know you're from a, um, crime family?" Was that what you called it?

"I don't know about *the Lockwoods*." Gia made air quotes with her fingers. "Ramirez seemed to know everything Susan knew about me." She refocused her gaze out the window. "Susan was my biological father's sister. Except I didn't know Franco wasn't my biological father until Ramirez called to tell me Susan had died."

"Where's your biological father?" Immediately, Aurora cursed herself for speaking without thinking. She'd never heard of Susan Lockwood having any family.

"Dead," Gia said with even less emotion than before.

It was like she was shutting down, and Aurora wished she could rewind. Return to holding Gia close, and come up with a better way to figure out what happened next.

"My father, I mean Franco, killed Susan's brother and my mother for having an affair. For trying to take me away. They tried to kidnap me. Or rescue me. I didn't know any of it at the time. I was only five, and the day is a blur. But if I'd known, I wouldn't have stayed. I shouldn't have stayed."

"Hey." Aurora rested a hand on Gia's shoulder, and she flinched. Aurora pretended that didn't cut deep. "Slow down. You escaped, and that's good."

"When it was easy. Even before I found out the truth, I shouldn't have sat around living off his money. I knew he killed people. Killing my mother and biological father shouldn't have been different than anyone else."

"Yes, it should. Of course hearing he killed your *mother* and a father you never knew would be different than knowing he was a killer in general."

Gia shrugged, like she disagreed but couldn't be bothered arguing. "I still stayed too long. And now they've found me."

"I'm not letting them take you, Gia. Fuck. I'd like to see

them try." Aurora might not have her body or her magic. She might be up shit creek with her own problems, but no one was laying a hand on Gia, least of all the man who'd killed her family.

Gia's hopeless expression didn't change. "They will try, Aurora. I might be useless to Franco, but he won't let me go. Not when my disappearance could make him look weak."

Aurora fumed, ice surging through her soul. *Unless?* She'd teach Franco a lesson straight from Hell for making Gia believe crap like that. "He's just a goon with a gun."

Gia scoffed. "Don't underestimate him. Franco has an army of goons with guns."

"So? You're a witch, surrounded by other witches. The Lockwoods will help you. I know they will. I'm surprised Susan didn't rally them to get you sooner. I know I said they aren't fighters, but they'll do anything to protect their own, and you're their family."

Gia remained unmoved. "Apparently, Susan tried to contact me. I don't know. It doesn't matter."

"Okay." There was a long pause. "Why didn't you tell me any of this before?"

Gia's expression pinched, and she looked away. "Because I'm not good like you. I'm complicit in everything my father has done. I never did anything about it. I ate food bought with blood money, lived in his mansion full of pretty things, let him care for me when I was ill. He killed my mother, and I accepted his sanctuary like a fool."

"Like a fool? You were a child. His actions aren't your responsibility. Even after you became an adult. I don't believe for a second you could have stopped him on your own. It wasn't solely up to you to do something. You might not have been bound like me, but humans don't need magic to control one another. I'm not better than you, Gia."

"But you fought back."

"No. I never stopped my family doing a damn thing. Not to others in my coven and not to anyone else. The reason the Thornfields don't have a stronger foothold in Shearwater Landing, enslaving humans or other witches, is that a bigger, badder coven of vampires is in power. It's nothing to do with me."

Gia choked on air, her eyes going wide. *"Vampires?"*

"Don't get distracted." Aurora floated closer, and Gia didn't flinch. A small relief. "I'm saying, all I could do was escape. Neither of us is complicit for not being able to stop the people who held us prisoner."

"But I didn't try. You literally left your body to get out. I waited for the perfect opportunity to land in my lap."

Aurora fixed her with a hard stare. "To me, it sounds like you discovered a truth that had been hidden from you, and you reacted to a new situation. That's perfectly reasonable."

Gia rubbed her temple, and Aurora took advantage of her lack of argument. "There's nothing wrong with needing help. What do you think I'm doing now? I took a risk and ended up needing help as much as ever. I don't see why either of us should have to do anything alone."

"You don't need to do this alone." Gia rubbed her head again and walked over to the coffee table to grab one of her pill bottles. "I feel terrible. It's sickening to think I lived there for twenty years after he killed her. And I...I think my brother knew."

Fuck. His betrayal seemed to hurt Gia as much as what her father had done. At least from what Aurora was picking up. "You have a brother?"

Gia swallowed a pill, chasing it with the dregs in a nearby water bottle. "Yeah, he's older. Heir to my father's empire. But Marc was always kind to me. God, that sounds pathetic."

"Gia, stop judging yourself. Latching onto kindness in a toxic environment is survival. Not pathetic."

Gia tossed the water bottle away. "Sure, but I'm furious about all of it. And, I don't know, it's easier to be angry at myself because at least I have control over fixing *me*. Of being a better person. I can't fix what Franco did. Can't make my brother care about anyone but himself. I can't bring my mother back, and I can't make Franco remorseful for what he's done. I can't take him down."

Aurora wanted to ask why not. Gia had such potential and an impressive amount of magical power. More than Aurora had, even with her body. But this wasn't about fighting or magic. Not right now. "You don't have to stop him. You can escape and take back *your* life. Those aren't small accomplishments. It's all I ever planned to do. I didn't plan to come for my family when I was free. I was never looking back."

Gia chewed her lip. "Same. I planned to sell up and disappear, but now it's too late."

Aurora wished Gia had asked the Lockwoods for help. They could have helped her deflect pursuers with magic before it had gotten to this point. "How did they find you?"

"Franco knew who my biological father was. It wouldn't take a genius to look into his extended family and find Susan. But I thought I had more time. No one knew what I'd discovered, and I hoped Franco wouldn't put it together right away. He must have been waiting for something like this to happen."

"Well, Franco and his goons are in for a rude awakening. We used magic against them today. They'll be pissing themselves. Confused. Running scared."

Salvator's quick recovery and lack of terror made Aurora pause. How had he held his own against the paranormal? It was difficult to imagine even a seasoned human criminal being unflappable in the face of a real-life ghost. But then, Aurora couldn't imagine what Salvator's life had been like. Maybe nothing fazed people like him.

"Do you think anyone else saw your magic?" Gia asked.

"You mean your magic." Aurora smiled, but Gia didn't follow suit. "I doubt it. The SUV blocked us, and to be honest, humans naturally frame anything they see within the confines of how they believe the world works. Unless it's impossible to ignore. All anyone would have seen was a man falling into a vehicle and shouting when he touched it."

"But you revealed yourself."

"In the bright sun. I bet people across the street didn't see more than a shiny ripple."

Gia frowned. "It's not like it matters now." She rubbed her head again. "Fuck, I think I'm getting a migraine."

Aurora wished they'd at least made it to the apothecary. "Do you need to lie down?"

"It wouldn't hurt." Gia settled on the couch, looking at the ceiling.

Aurora floated above her, hovering flat on her stomach in a mirror of Gia's position.

Gia smiled at last. "Thanks. Now I don't even have to turn my head."

Aurora echoed her smile. "No problem. Feel free to close your eyes."

Gia did, lines creasing her forehead and betraying how far from relaxed she really was. "I can't deal with this right now."

"You mean a headache?"

"A migraine. If I black out and Salvator returns, we're screwed."

Fuck, they really should have run somewhere else, but returning here had been reflexive. Aurora hadn't questioned it at the time.

"I was bound to get a migraine when I couldn't afford it.

That's the other reason I stayed. I believed I couldn't cope on my own."

Aurora's brow furrowed. "People get migraines all the time. I'm not trying to minimize your experience, but it seems like a manageable condition."

"You'd think. But what happens to me is different. No one can explain it."

Which was why Gia had asked if it could be magic.

The temperature in the room seemed to drop, and a sense of foreboding snuck up on Aurora. No, Gia couldn't be cursed. Lilly had checked. Gia's father was a mobster, not a witch. A rare medical condition wasn't out of the realm of possibility, but Aurora's regret over not making it to the apothecary doubled.

"How long until the pills take effect?" she asked.

Gia shrugged, eyes still closed. "Depends. They don't always work."

"Did the stress of today trigger it? Should I stop talking?"

Gia cracked an eye open. "You can talk. Stress isn't always a trigger. I didn't get a headache the night I ran away, even though I was stressed. Sam drove for days without stopping." She paused. "Was she using magic?"

"I don't know Sam personally, but not needing much sleep is a vampire thing."

Gia hummed thoughtfully. "Weird. Sam didn't fry in the sun... I think it's getting worse."

She must mean the headache, which had to be terrible if even discussing vampires was on the back burner. Aurora would explain the realities versus myths later. "What can I do? Should we call Lilly?"

A sharp tapping sounded on the door, and they both froze.

Aurora drifted over and checked through the peephole. "It's the neighbor." A flare of annoyance sparked in her chest.

Gia groaned. "Pretend no one's home."

Viv knocked again, but after a minute, she gave up and disappeared. Aurora returned to the couch.

"How are you feeling?"

"Not great." Gia sat up, a determined set to her jaw. "But we should move while I'm functional. Get out of here and hide from Salvator. My family used my condition to trap me, but they were wrong. I can find a way deal with this."

Aurora floated closer. "We'll get through it, I promise."

Gia gave her a thin smile. "Let's try the apothecary."

Aurora nodded. "Can you book a ride? Lilly could meet us there, and we can figure out where to go next."

Gia stood. "I don't have a credit card, so I can't use any rideshare apps. I suppose I could call a taxi and pay cash."

"Let's do that." Aurora flew over to the window to see if Trey or Salvator were lurking. She spotted no one.

"I might lose consciousness while we're out. If I do, will you be able to help?" Fear flitted across Gia's already strained expression. It hurt to see, but she was bringing her worries to Aurora, being vulnerable, and Aurora wouldn't let her down.

"I'll be there with you. Being a ghost isn't ideal, but I promise I'll everything in my power to keep you safe."

Gia cocked her head. "Do you think you could, you know, go inside me and control me while I'm unconscious?"

Aurora jolted. "It's one thing to channel your power when you're aware. We connected by accident. I'd never invade you."

Gia gave her a pained smile and stood. "I know. You have my permission, so it's not an invasion. Worst comes to worst, you're free to take over."

"Really?" The trust shocked Aurora, especially after how guarded Gia had been since they met.

"Yes, really. I like the sound of channeling, rather than possessing. Like you're helping me rather than hijacking me to do your bidding."

"That would be despicable."

"Is something like that possible?"

"Witches can't possess people, but we can channel each other. Usually, it requires a blood exchange and goes both ways. Since I'm not in my body, things are a bit haywire."

Aurora had never thought she'd power-share with another witch. Most witches didn't. Even the Nightingales, who were into blood magic, didn't channel. They stuck to using someone's blood like a spell ingredient so the caster wouldn't have to give anything in exchange. It was a nasty practice, and had made Aurora suspicious of any kind of power sharing until now.

With Gia, sharing was another thing entirely. If Aurora had her magic in this form, she wouldn't hesitate to lend it.

"I'll feel better knowing you can step in if we need it," Gia said as she went over to the kitchen, grabbed all the cash from the cereal box, and shoved it in her backpack.

Aurora's chest expanded. "Of course. And when this is all over, I'll teach you to use your magic yourself."

Gia opened a door leading to a laundry nook and grabbed what appeared to be more cash from behind the washer. "I'm a long way off doing anything with magic. But yeah. You should teach me when we aren't running around hiding. Let me grab the rest of this"—she waved the thick stack of money—"and we can go."

SEVENTEEN

GIA

THE ACHE in her head was getting worse, but Gia did her best to push through it. Normally, she'd never risk doing anything once the pain got to this point, but she wasn't sitting around waiting for Salvator to return, even knowing Aurora could take over and wield her magic.

As far as she knew, no spell could stop a bullet.

Franco wouldn't want her killed, but accidents happened when guns were involved, especially if Aurora threw magic into the mix. It was a miracle Salvator had kept his cool earlier.

Gia had to take this step. Take action. Manage her migraines herself as best she could. There was nothing weak about needing rest or doing things differently, but this wasn't a normal situation. She had to stay away from Salvator, even if going out now rather than resting cost her.

Hopefully, the apothecary could help, and when she felt better, she'd see the situation with fresh eyes and figure out what to do next.

Gia exited her building, sunglasses on, and Aurora invisible by her side.

"Hey, Gia," Viv called, hurrying to catch up to her before the front door closed.

What the hell was with this woman? "Viv. I've gotta run, sorry. Car's here." Gia pointed to the idling taxi.

"Oh, a yellow cab. How vintage. I love it." Viv gave an airy laugh before narrowing her eyes in Gia's direction. "Are you all right? You seemed freaked out earlier. And with that guy who's been hanging around..." She raised a brow.

Gia's heart skipped, her head pounding to match. "Have you seen him again?"

"Nah." Viv waved a hand. She looked like she was dressed for the gym again, though something about the all-black aesthetic was giving thief-in-the-night vibes. "I haven't seen him since last night."

"Awesome. I've really gotta run." Gia ducked into the cab without giving Viv a chance to reply, and shut her eyes briefly as she suppressed a groan.

This apothecary better have a magic cure.

A tiny spark tickled her hand, like Aurora was trying to comfort her, or remind her she was there, and Gia's heart clenched. Not being alone gave her strength.

She hadn't been her best self this afternoon, and Aurora hadn't batted an eye. Maybe it was because they were stuck together and Aurora couldn't run if she wanted to, but Gia couldn't help believing it went deeper.

The taxi pulled out, and the driver confirmed the address where they were headed. Gia should have watched for cars, kept on the lookout for Salvator or Franco's other men, not to mention Trey. But looking hurt, so Gia kept her eyes closed, trusting Aurora to be her lookout, accepting the help and doing her best not to feel guilty about it.

"There's a truck double-parked ahead," the cabbie said after a while. "Can I drop you here?"

Had they arrived already? Gia opened her eyes. The cab had pulled over at a side street, and sure enough, the way ahead was blocked by a truck.

"Here's fine." Gia gritted her teeth against the pain as she paid and added a generous tip. She slid out of the cab, making sure to hold the door open long enough for Aurora to slip out unseen.

"We're halfway down the block from The Herb Emporium. It's across the street. Green building," Aurora's disembodied voice whispered.

Gia nodded, spotting the place easily with its faded green sign. The street was lined with shops, but she didn't have the energy to take it all in as she began searching for a gap in traffic. At a lull, she crossed and hurried along the block.

"Gia!" a familiar voice yelled, and she froze.

"Who's he?" Aurora hissed.

Gia turned, knowing before she caught sight of him. "My brother."

Marc stood merely five feet away. As far as Gia could see, he was alone, the driver's door of an unfamiliar car standing open behind him.

"Are you following me?" Gia asked, words sharper than she'd expected.

Marc's steps faltered, his eyes widening. "G, I'm here to help. We've got to get home." He took two careful steps closer.

Her voice rose. "Are you kidding me? Home?" Gia's headache flared, but for once, the pain was an afterthought. "To the man who killed our mother?"

Marc's face fell, but he didn't seem the least bit surprised, and he didn't contradict her. "Gia..."

"No, don't *Gia* me," she snapped. "You knew? And you went along with it? Became just like him?"

"Hey, I'm not just like Father. You know there are things I'd do differently. Will do differently when it's my turn, but *come on*, Gia. Live in reality. Our mother wasn't a saint."

"And our father belongs in Hell. Though he's not actually my father, is he?"

"*Gia!*" Marc somehow managed to look offended.

So, he knew that part too. She fumed, fists clenched. "Where are all your men, huh? You never go anywhere alone."

Marc swiped a hand over his face. "They don't know I'm here. Look, I'm taking a risk right now. For you. There isn't much time. Come with me, and we can work something out. I know what happened with Salvator earlier."

He did? How was he not freaking out? Guess he had a better poker face than Gia gave him credit for.

Gia's voice dropped to a growl. "Then you know you don't have any power over me. Leave me alone, or I'll toss you aside and burn more than your hand."

Marc's face bloomed with splotches of red. "I'm your brother. Your *family*. How dare you?"

"How dare you talk to me after lying to me my entire life. You knew, Marco. And you didn't care."

Marc surged forward, his voice raised. "What do you know about how I feel?"

"Hey, what's going on here?" a tall, Latino man asked, his hard stare fixed on Marc.

Marc puffed out his chest, adjusting the sleeve of his suit jacket. "None of your business."

"No?" The man crossed his arms, muscles bulging. "Last I checked, what happens on this street is my business. I suggest you take your shit elsewhere."

"Fine. Gia, let's go." Marc gestured to the car.

Gia turned away and walked past the random guy without glancing at him. She was grateful for the interruption, but so fucking tired of needing people to step in.

"Wait," Aurora's disembodied voice hissed, and Gia realized she'd walked past the apothecary.

She doubled back and ducked into the faded green shop. The scent of herbs filled her nose, and her head pounded. Would Marc follow?

The door opened behind her, bell ringing as someone else entered. "Do you need help?"

Gia turned to see the man from the street staring at her, his gaze much warmer than it had been, but she wasn't comforted. "Are you following me?"

He maneuvered carefully around her. "No, this is my shop."

She registered his stained apron as he slid behind the counter. "Oh."

"So, can I help? Or are you browsing?"

Maybe Gia should relax, but between the budding migraine and Marc, it was impossible. "You're a witch?"

The man nodded. "And so are you."

Gia's gut twisted. It was so weird how they could tell. She'd need to ask Aurora how to detect witches herself. "Is that why you intervened outside? Because I'm a witch?"

"No." He shrugged. "It looked like trouble, and like I said, trouble doesn't fly around here. I'm Nico, by the way."

This was the man who was friends with the Lockwoods. Gia took a reluctant step closer to the counter, wishing Aurora were visible so they could confer. So she didn't have to face this unknown witch without a clue what she was doing.

"A friend recommended I come here," she began.

Nico nodded, waiting patiently for her to go on.

"I'm not, um, I haven't known about magic long, but I get really bad migraines and was wondering if you had anything for pain?"

Nico turned toward a well-stocked shelf on the wall behind

him, perusing the vast array of tiny bottles. "Sure do. Have you tried any potions before?"

"No. I didn't know about witches until I met one recently. I brought the pills I usually take, if that's relevant?"

Nico selected two bottles and set them on the counter. "May I see them?"

Gia extracted the bottle from her backpack, careful not to let the cash show.

Nico took it. "This isn't a standard label."

It seemed normal to Gia, but she'd been taking these pills for years.

"May I open it?" Nico asked.

Gia nodded, and he unscrewed the lid, shaking a few pills onto the counter. He frowned, a deep crease forming on his brow.

"Mixing magic and human medication can be risky," he ventured.

"I can stop taking the pills while I try a magic solution. Are those potions?" She pointed to the little bottles.

"These?" Nico looked confused. "Yes, they're potions. But I meant mixing magic with the pills, like you've been doing."

"Like I've been *what*?" Gia couldn't help glancing to the side, as if Aurora would explain. A comforting spark nudged her shoulder, but no clarity came with it.

"These pills—which appear pretty garden variety—have been altered with magic."

"*What?*" Gia repeated, her head throbbing anew.

"You didn't know?" Nico scrubbed a hand over his face. "Melanie?" he called, and a woman popped out from behind a curtain that must have led to another room.

"Yes?" she said.

"Can you examine this for me?" He handed over one of the pills.

"Sure thing." Melanie grabbed it and disappeared again.

"Those pills can't have magic," Gia protested, her sluggish brain doing its best to keep up. "They're from a human doctor. The prescription gets filled at a regular pharmacy."

"Prescription? They look like over-the-counter painkillers to me. Do you pick them up yourself?"

"No." She'd always had people to run errands for her, at her father's insistence, but that was an image thing. "I know they're the same shape as other pills, but they're not *the same* as the over-the-counter stuff. They can't be."

Anger flared, and Gia's head bloomed with pain. Not every pill looked completely unique to the average person. He must be wrong.

Nico studied the remaining pills on the counter, picking them up one at a time. He set one aside. "This one doesn't seem to have any magic to it, but the others do. Would you mind letting me inspect the rest?"

Gia dumped the pills on the counter. "My family doesn't know about magic. I've only ever been to regular doctors, so I don't see how there could be magic in any of them."

"Perhaps the person who fills the prescription messed with them without your family's knowledge. Most of these are unmagical, but these"—he nudged another pill into a growing pile—"have all been altered."

"But why are they mixed with non-altered ones?" Even if, say, the doctor or pharmacist was a secret witch, trying to help with magic pills, wouldn't they all be the same? Gia had never added pills from one bottle into another.

"I don't know." Nico's frown deepened. "I'm sorry to spring this on you, but it's good you're here. We'll figure out what the magic does and get you something else to help your headaches. I'll be right back."

Nico disappeared behind the curtain.

"Are you sure your family doesn't know about magic?" Aurora hissed.

"Yes." Of course they didn't know. If Franco knew about magic, he'd have far more power than he did already. "Didn't Lilly check me for magic? I'd taken a pill within the two weeks."

"She checked for spells cast on *you*. Magic acting on a secondary item alters the item, not you. It wouldn't have been detectable unless you'd been in the process of taking a pill when she checked."

Fuck, but before Gia could respond, the curtain shifted, and Nico reappeared, looking grim.

"Melanie did a basic analysis. Something more thorough will take more time, but she can already tell the spell wasn't meant to enhance the pill's effects."

"Meaning what? Explain it to me like I learned about magic yesterday."

"Yesterday? All right. If someone was trying to help your headaches, they'd cast a spell to increase the painkiller's effectiveness, but this spell seems to do the opposite."

"The opposite." Goddamn, she'd turned into a parrot. Apparently, this was her breaking point.

Nico nodded, nothing but serious. "I'm afraid so. Wherever these pills came from, the person who messed with them was using them to make your headaches worse."

Gia gripped the counter as dread welled within her. "Could the spell make me black out? Take my memory?"

Nico's eyes went wide. "No. Witches can't alter memories. A spell could make you black out, but from what Melanie is picking up, it's a pain trigger and nothing more."

Sometimes the pills worked, and sometimes they didn't. Sometimes her headaches got worse even if she took them.

Gia's knuckles turned white as she gripped the counter

harder. That was why they were mixed. It was a crapshoot. The pills worked enough to keep her taking them. But sometimes, they made her worse. On purpose.

Why would Franco do this to her? Because she couldn't believe this was a coincidence, or some other malevolent force. Franco must know about magic after all. Something like this didn't happen under his nose without his knowledge. He was always two steps ahead.

Marc hadn't been shocked to hear Salvator had seen a ghost or been burned inexplicably. He must know about magic, too. Did he know about the pills? Was he...

"Was the guy yelling at me outside a witch?" Gia asked.

Nico seemed thrown by the change in topic, but recovered quickly. "No. He was human."

"You checked?" She had to be sure.

"I did. Was he the one to give you the pills?"

"No. Never mind." She had to figure out why her father would play games, making her headaches worse, when she already had intense blackouts and memory loss that couldn't be due to the tainted pills.

Wasn't her condition bad enough? Or did Franco need her to believe she was even sicker than she was? And if Franco knew about magic...had her mother? She had to talk to the damn lawyer. See what Susan had told him before her death.

"I'll take the potions, thanks." Gia pointed to Nico's selections.

"Of course. Do you have anyone to help you deal with what you've learned? Are you safe from whoever gave you these pills?"

It was kind to ask, but Gia wasn't banking on this random guy's help. "I know the Lockwood Coven. They'll help."

Nico nodded. "They're good people. If you need something

else, I'll be here." He explained a few things about the potions and how they worked, then rang her up.

It was time to hear out the Lockwoods.

After Nico confirmed it would counteract the spell on the tainted pills, Gia took a swig of one of the potions and left the apothecary. Marc seemed to have disappeared from the vicinity, and no one jumped out at her as she waited for a cab and made her escape.

Gia's headache faded, and by the time the taxi pulled over in front of the lawyer's building, her pain was gone. Seemed the pill she'd taken earlier was one of the tainted ones.

It was a wonder smoke didn't billow from her ears. Gia felt like taking a bat to every single one of Franco and Marc's sports cars, then turning her fury on them, pummeling them until there was nothing left.

They'd been making her sicker. Lying to her about even more than she'd thought. All to some mysterious end she couldn't fathom. Unless it was nothing more than cruelty. Punishment for being a bastard.

Why not dispose of her like they did her mother? It almost would have been kinder.

Gia climbed out of the cab, holding the door for the invisible Aurora. Whatever was happening, she was getting to the bottom of it and claiming her retribution. Escaping was nowhere near enough. Not anymore.

Would Aurora understand her change of heart?

The cab sped off, and Aurora's disembodied voice piped up. "Are you okay with me showing myself once we're inside?"

Gia blinked out of her rage-fog. "Of course."

"Lilly already told the rest of the coven, so it shouldn't be a shock for Edward or Grace to see me."

"Good. I'd rather talk to you openly."

Soft tingles trailed along Gia's arm, at odds with the hardness creeping into Aurora's tone. "Come on, let's go figure out who we need to smite." It seemed she understood.

They entered the building, and Gia hiked up the stairs and into the office suite. "I need to speak to Edward Ramirez urgently."

The receptionist, Grace, glanced up from behind her desk like she'd been caught off guard. Her smile didn't falter. "Gia, hello." There was a flicker of light beside Gia, and Grace gasped. "And Aurora." Her hand fluttered to her chest. "Damnation, hearing what happened and seeing it are two different things."

"What the hell is *that*?" came a shout behind them.

Gia stiffened. She hadn't noticed anyone else here, and apparently, neither had Aurora. Turning, she faced the small waiting area where Viv, of all damn people, sat on a worn sofa.

Unease curled in Gia's gut. Why was she always popping up?

Viv stood, attention fixed on Aurora like she was fascinated rather than terrified. "Are you a ghost?"

Aurora didn't bother stating the obvious. "You know about magic, I'm guessing?" she said blandly.

Viv shrugged. "Sure do. If you need to talk to Mr. Ramirez, I don't mind waiting. Even though I have an appointment."

"Um. Thanks." Gia glanced at Grace, who gestured to the door.

"Go on in. I'm sure Edward will be happy to help."

Gia pushed Viv from her mind—she was a mystery for another time—and entered the office, Aurora at her elbow.

Inside, the lawyer sat at his desk, the room as cluttered and candle-strewn as ever.

"Sounds like you're causing a commotion," Edward said by way of greeting. "How can I help, Gia? And Aurora. I'm so sorry to hear what the Thornfields were planning for you."

"Thanks, but we're not here for me." Aurora floated toward the desk, and Gia shut the office door.

She got straight to the point. "Do my family—the Balzanos—know about magic?"

Edward folded his hands on his desk. "Yes, they do."

Gia plopped into the chair facing him. "I had no idea."

"I'm sorry. Susan hoped you might, but feared you'd be unaware. I didn't want to try to enlighten you before we met in person."

A logical move. Gia wouldn't have believed him or returned his call if he'd started yammering on about magic. She'd still be in Ashton Lakes if he'd told her she was a witch.

"Wait," Aurora said before Gia could respond. "How do you know the Balzanos are aware of magic?"

Edward sighed. Not in annoyance, rather like he regretted what he had to say. "It goes back to Jeffrey and Letti's attempt to bring you here, Gia. As far as anyone can tell, the Balzanos weren't aware of magic then. Your mother hadn't been before meeting Jeffrey. But he must have used magic in the fight that resulted in his and Letti's deaths. Jeffrey's unconfirmed death, I should say, since there's no official record. Anyway. By the time Susan figured out something terrible happened to her brother, it seems Franco had wised up. A spell was cast to prevent Susan from reaching you by any means, Gia. Susan spent decades trying to find a way around it."

Decades? Gia hadn't even known the woman existed, and she'd been fighting for her all this time? Her heart ached, but the story still didn't add up. "Franco can't have cast a spell. If my brother Marc isn't a witch, Franco can't be either."

"He doesn't have to possess magical ability himself," Edward said patiently. "Franco could have hired a witch once he discovered magic. He'd have had time between your mother's failed escape and when Susan first attempted to get involved to seek someone out."

"Okay, but how could a spell keep Susan away? You got me out without any trouble. Too easily, even."

"The spell stopping Susan was linked to your bloodline. Meaning Susan, as a blood relative, couldn't get to you. She founded this coven in part to try to save you, to bring her brother's daughter home, but all our attempts failed because the coven's magic was intertwined with Susan as our founder, and therefore deflected by the spell. When Susan died, taking away the blood-link between you and the Lockwood Coven, we could finally reach you."

Gia looked at Aurora, too stunned to speak. Did this make sense? Aurora didn't seem confused, so it must add up.

Aurora reached for Gia and brushed their fingers together, sending sparks up Gia's arm. "Tell him the rest," Aurora coaxed.

Right, Gia had to keep going, take everything in, and move forward so she could figure out how to stop her father. And make him pay.

"I just found out the pills I take for a rare medical condition were altered by magic to make it worse," she told him.

He scowled. "I'm so sorry."

"I guess Franco hired a witch to do that, too. But why? The more I learn, the more *everything* seems like a lie. What if I'm not even sick? What if my memory loss is magic? It seems too convenient not to be. I don't remember the day Jeffrey tried to take me. I always thought it was because I was young, and I'd blocked out the trauma, or because my condition set in a few years later, and everything became so murky. Of course, old memories might fade away. But now, it's nothing but suspicious."

"Spells can't take your memories the way they can make your headaches worse," Aurora said again. "Lilly checked, and you haven't been cursed."

The sound of voices swelled outside, and the door burst open. Gia spun in her seat, finding Viv in the doorway.

"You can't go in there," Grace said from behind her.

Viv ignored her. "Sorry to interrupt," she said without a shred of remorse. "But you're looking at this all wrong."

Edward stood from his seat. "This conversation is confidential."

"It's fine. Gia is a friend, and I couldn't sit around and let you miss the obvious. You all are forgetting about vampires."

"I was not forgetting about vampires," Edward said, his tone harsh. "I was about to say, a vampire could mess with your memory, Gia."

"What?" She looked at Aurora.

Her cheeks paled, almost disappearing entirely. "Vampire hypnosis didn't even cross my mind. It wouldn't have explained your pain, and we were focused on a spell that could physically hurt you to the point of blacking out. We thought the memory loss was a symptom of the blackouts. But the blackouts on their own... The gaps in memory... Fuck. Now that we know the pills were making your headaches worse, it's obvious the pain is a separate issue."

"So you're saying a *vampire* was stealing my memory?" Gia glanced around at them all.

"One very well could have been." Edward tapped his chin with a finger. "Is there anyone associated with the Balzanos who seems to age particularly well, to the point they might not be aging at all?"

Gia's mouth dropped open, about to deny it. She stilled. "Everyone says Franco looks as good now as he did a decade ago. But he's aged since then. He must have. This is ridiculous." The man she'd always known as her father wasn't a vampire.

"There's one way to know for sure." Viv couldn't seem to help butting in. "I can remove the hypnosis, revealing who cast it."

"*You?*" Gia frowned at her. "Wait. If I've been hypnotized, why didn't Lilly detect it?"

Viv rolled her eyes like everyone was being incredibly silly. "Vampire hypnosis isn't a spell and doesn't physically affect your body. It's all in the mind. *Illusion.* It's not witch magic."

Gia still didn't follow. "Then how can you remove it? Aren't you a witch?"

Viv smiled, her canines elongating into fangs. "I'm a vampire."

Gia should have been shocked, but she'd passed that point several revelations ago. She'd process vampires and Viv later. She clearly didn't know the first thing about real vampires, considering Viv was out in broad daylight. Whatever. There was no time to dwell. She needed answers, or she might start screaming and never stop.

"Do it. Remove the hypnosis."

"Gia, you don't know what you'll find." Aurora's voice rose in alarm, concern lining her flickering expression.

"But I can't not know. I can't keep wondering. I'm tired of being cautious all the fucking time."

Aurora smiled sadly. "I know, baby. But take a second to think about what you might uncover. It sounds like there are tons of gaps in your memory, and your family is terrible. Someone erased more than the day your mother died."

"I know. I can't bear the thought of someone stealing so much..." Gia's stomach cramped, and she worried she'd be sick.

Fifteen years of gaps and a fog. Gia didn't know herself. Her own story. Nothing would be right until she put the pieces together.

"We'll start small." Viv came farther into the room on silent feet. Some of her earlier flare dimmed, but not quite bringing her to the point of somberness. "Let me check you for mind alterations first. Then, I can start undoing them. If you want."

Gia nodded.

"Grace, can you reschedule the rest of my afternoon?" Edward asked, and she nodded, leaving the room. "We can call one of the vampires in the coven to help. The Lockwoods are a hybrid group. Viv doesn't have to be involved."

Gia realized he was talking to her. "Viv can do it. I don't want to wait. Unless," Gia looked at Viv suspiciously. "Do you think she'll hurt me?"

To her credit, Viv didn't seem at all offended as she glanced at Edward, awaiting his verdict.

"I didn't mean to cast suspicion." Edward returned to his seat. "Viv is here to see me about joining the Lockwood Coven. I don't have reason to believe she'll hurt you, but I don't know her on a personal level yet."

"I won't bite. Promise." Viv pouted. "Besides, if I did anything shady, you'd find out quick enough. Why would I risk it? I want in with the Lockwoods, and what better way than to help you? I've been trying to help all along, and you kept pushing me away."

Could anyone blame her? Viv hadn't been forthcoming, which made sense if she had been trying to sus Gia out before revealing herself as a vampire. And it wasn't like Gia trusted easily. For good fucking reason.

But none of that mattered right now.

"Do it. I need to know, and the sooner the better." Gia gripped the arms of her chair. The people here weren't the ones hurting her. The Lockwoods never wanted to do anything but help.

The Balzanos, on the other hand, never wanted what was best for her, and she'd known that all along.

NINETEEN

GIA

GIA: Age Five.

GIA ARRIVED at the park with Ma, just the two of them. Marc was at his friend's house, and Daddy was busy. He was always busy, but Gia didn't mind. She secretly liked Ma better, even though she wasn't supposed to like one parent more than the other. Ma was never mean. Never scary.

"We're going to meet my friend all the way over by the trees," Ma said as they walked away from the car.

"Ugh. That's far," Gia whined, even though she liked the trees.

"I know, sweetie. Once we get there, we're going for a ride. It was a surprise, so I didn't tell you before. We're going on a secret trip."

Gia jumped, clapping her hands, all annoyance about the long walk forgotten. "Just you and me?"

"You and me, and my friend, Jeff."

"Okay." Gia had met Jeff before. He was as nice as Ma and did the best magic tricks.

They walked across the huge park, over the grass, past the playground and soccer field, on and on. It wasn't a bad walk, but Ma didn't seem to be having fun yet. She looked over her shoulder again and again.

Gia hated when Ma was scared. It scared her, even if she didn't know what was wrong.

At last, they reached the trees, and Ma looked around one more time before continuing on.

"Where's Jeff? I thought we were meeting here."

"A little farther, Gia, sweetie." Ma scooped her up, cradling her against her chest as she kept walking.

They came upon a back road. Gia had never been this far into the trees and didn't even know cars could drive through here. Going into the forest was usually out of bounds when they went to the park.

A car was parked on the road with its rear door open. They reached it, and Ma slid right in, closing the door behind her as she kept Gia tucked close.

"Hey," Jeff said from the driver's seat as he pulled away from the curb.

"Wait! We don't have our seatbelts on!" Gia cried. The car was moving!

"I'll buckle you in." Ma set her in a car seat and quickly did the buckle.

"You're not safe," Gia protested. Ma didn't have her seatbelt fastened, and she'd told Gia to *never* be in a moving car without one on.

"Here." Ma buckled in. Her smile didn't look happy. "See, we're both safe."

Gia wasn't so sure. Jeff drove fast, like Daddy did sometimes, and Ma didn't like speeding. She wasn't convinced this trip would be fun anymore.

GIA GASPED, her eyes popping open. She was in Edward Ramirez's office, a twenty-five-year-old woman, but her childhood self felt so close she could still taste the innocent confusion.

"Gia." Aurora was in front of her, face fearful, her form flickering in and out. "Breathe."

Gia was crying. When had she started crying?

The rest of the memory flooded her mind. The car that had smashed into them. Flashes of light. An explosion. The yelling. Gunshots. Franco standing over Jeffrey. Her mother bleeding in the street. Salvator pulling her from the smashed car as she screamed bloody murder.

"I remember them killing her," she told Aurora. "I was there. I didn't go to the park with the nanny. Ma took me. To run away."

"They must have planted part of a false memory," Viv said, and Gia jumped. She'd forgotten the vampire completely. "Giving you something to remember is less suspicious than a complete hole."

Sure. Fine. But knowing Viv had been in her head, Gia wanted to get as far away from her as she could. "Can you see what I'm remembering?"

"No," Viv said more gently than Gia thought she was capable of. "I can see evidence of the hypnosis well enough to undo it, but I can't see what I'm uncovering. Do you want me to keep going?"

Gia nodded, marginally reassured.

"I'll try my best to work from oldest to newest. Unless there's a time you want me to focus on?"

Gia's heart sank, and it had been pretty low to begin with. "There's a lot missing, isn't there?"

Viv grimaced. "I've never seen someone with such a heavily altered mind."

Aurora made a small, pained sound. "I'm so sorry, Gia."

She wanted to fall into Aurora, kick everyone out of the room, and talk to her alone, share all of her frantic thoughts, ask *why*, even when she didn't expect an answer. But she couldn't be derailed from her task, or she might never return to it.

"Can we uncover the first memory blackout?" she asked Viv. "Is that the next oldest one? Can you tell?"

Viv fixed her gaze on Gia, eyes glowing as her vampire power flared. "There's a tangle of altered memories before we get to the first complete erasure."

The holes in Gia's memory loomed like wraiths, threatening to drag her down. She needed them gone, even if she didn't want to know. But things already didn't make sense. There was no reason to make it harder for herself by jumping around and targeting her first blackout if there was more to uncover from her younger days.

"Is it possible to uncover things in chronological order?"

Viv promised to do her best and brought Gia into a trance-like state, her glowing eyes blurring and fading away, the rest of the office melting along with them.

Scenes flashed before Gia. Franco talking about what happened in the park. Mentions of Jeffrey that she'd caught while men talked around her. Franco discussing a new strategy to advance his position in the organization. Memories of her mother. The day she met Jeffrey. All the times he'd popped into her childhood before that fateful day.

So many little details had been smoothed out and replaced with mundane alternatives. It was a thorough cover-up, and a small miracle that any hint of Jeffrey Lockwood had escaped the purge. If Gia hadn't made a habit of listening outside doors undetected, she wouldn't have had a single clue.

As the memories unfurled, Gia got progressively older. The only constant was Franco, a figure on the periphery of each scene, but never the direct focus. He didn't address Gia at all until one memory surfaced. This was no longer something altered, but a picture she knew in her gut had been completely erased.

GIA: Ten Years Old.

SHE SAT on a hard chair in a huge, unfamiliar, empty room, Franco in front of her, his eyes glowing orange.

"Gianna, my dear, it's time to get started."

"I don't want—"

"Don't speak," Franco ordered, and her words clogged in her throat. "Don't move," he added.

And Gia couldn't. It was as if Franco's words held her spellbound, controlling her. She couldn't even lift a pinky or shake her head. Dread settled over her, almost as potent as the bone-deep confusion that plagued her ever since they got here.

"Don't worry. You won't remember," Franco said blandly, flicking open a pocket knife. "Hold out your hand."

She desperately wanted to disobey. To run away and never return. But the strange power held her without mercy, and her hand was drawn out in front of her, like it belonged to someone else.

Franco cut her palm, and she screamed.

"Silence!"

Gia's voice shriveled. What was happening to her? Why were her father's eyes glowing? Was this a dream? *Please let it be a dream. Please let me wake up.*

She didn't wake.

Franco swiped at her bloody palm with a finger and brought it to his mouth, opening wide. Sharp fangs that Gia had never seen before caught the light. The urge to scream had her wanting to crawl out of her skin, but Franco's commands held firm. She couldn't make a sound or move a muscle. All she could do was watch as Franco put his finger in his mouth, tasting her blood.

"I told you feeding isn't necessary," said a deep voice from behind Franco.

Gia strained to see and could barely make out an unfamiliar man standing at the edge of the illuminated area, half cast in shadow.

"How could I pass up a taste of the magic given to her by the *fool* who thought he could steal my wife?"

There was a heavy sigh. "Hypnosis will be enough to control her. Now that you know the spells, you can cast them through her. Command her magic as you command her voice, her body, but you must get her to repeat the spells. She must call on her magic, and you must tell her to do so."

"Yes, yes. We've been over this."

The man continued as if he hadn't been interrupted, sounding dangerously bored in the face of Franco's short temper. "Once you're adept at hypnosis, you can prep her and issue nonverbal commands, causing her to act out predesignated spells with nothing more than a wave of your hand or snap of your fingers."

She? Were they talking about her? Magic wasn't real. But then why couldn't she speak? If this were a dream, why wasn't she waking up?

"Salvator, bring in the first subject," Franco ordered.

A door opened and closed behind Gia, and her heart skipped. The sound of footsteps echoed through the room, and

Franco slowly rotated her chair, the legs scraping along the concrete floor.

Salvator emerged from the shadows, dragging a man Gia had seen among her father's friends. At least, she'd thought it had been among Franco's friends. She must have been wrong because the man was bound and bruised.

"My father will skin you alive for this," the man spat, struggling against his bindings.

Salvator kicked him in the stomach, and he doubled over. "This better work, boss." He kicked the man closer to where Gia sat. "Nabbing this little shit just started a war."

"One we will win." Franco put a hand on Gia's shoulder. "It will take everyone a while to figure out it wasn't the Russians who took poor Rosco's son. And by then, I'll have the support I need to take over. Once Rosco is out of the way."

Salvator nodded.

"You're deluded!" the bound man yelled. "You don't know what you're up against. You're no one. Disposable grunts. You can't overthrow my father."

"I can if I have magic." Franco's hand tightened painfully, and his face filled Gia's vision. "Look at me."

It was an odd request. She already was.

Her father's eyes flared orange once more. "Find the power within you, harness it, and repeat after me."

A string of nonsense words followed, and Gia was overcome with the sense of something swelling inside her. *What is that? What did the power within* mean?

She repeated the words as she'd been told.

Before Gia could get a handle on the sensation swelling in her gut, something within her burst forth. She couldn't see it, and would have thought she'd imagined it, but somehow, she knew it was real. It felt alive, this invisible thing, as it twisted to the shape of words her father had chosen.

The man on the floor screamed so loud, Gia's ears rang.

After a moment, he stopped, his voice hoarse as he whimpered.

"Excellent," Franco said, and Salvator smiled.

Tears streamed down Gia's face. Had she...?

"Look at me, Gia," Franco commanded, and she obeyed. "Find the power within and repeat after me."

It happened again. And again. Terrible things befell the man on the floor each time. Blood ran from his eyes, his nose. He turned ashen, cuts appearing on his skin out of nowhere.

Gia wanted desperately to look away. To run. To stop because *she* was doing these things. That living, pulsing *thing* inside her was doing it, guided by the words her father put in her mouth.

Gia could hardly see through her silent tears as the man finally died. Her mind was anything but silent. It had never been so loud, and Gia didn't think she'd survive it.

"Now, Gia." Franco crouched in front of her. "It's time to forget."

TWENTY
AURORA

Aurora watched helplessly as Gia thrashed in the chair. "Stop!"

Viv whirled around, eyes glowing. "I'm not doing anything. The memories I released are flooding her consciousness. I can't stop them now."

Satan on a stick, this was bad. Aurora had thought she'd been prepared. She thought she'd imagined the worst, but whatever Gia was seeing was something else altogether.

Agony twisted Gia's face, her eyes blank and streaming with tears as she saw things Aurora couldn't.

Whoever had done this was Aurora's number one enemy. Screw the Thornfields. At least they'd never tortured her like this.

"Gia, can you hear me?" Aurora ran a delicate finger along Gia's cheek, unable to wipe her tears away.

Gia gasped at the touch, and her eyes focused for a split second before her pupils blew wide. "Aurora?"

"It's me. You're okay. You're safe. Whatever you're seeing is a memory." Aurora's hands jumped from Gia's tear-stained face to her shoulders, to her wrists, and she had never been so bereft that they couldn't touch beyond tingles and sparks.

"I know who it was," Gia gasped, reaching for Aurora, their hands passing through each other.

"Who was it? Who did this?"

Gia wiped her bloodshot eyes. "Franco Balzano."

Heat flared deep in Aurora's soul. "And what did he do? What does he need to pay for?"

Gia's broken expression hardened. "Too many things to count."

"Still, a list would be nice," Viv butted in, sounding as glib as only a vampire could at a time like this.

"We'll all help deal with this, Gia," Edward added with far more compassion.

Gia seemed startled by the offer. "You'll help even if it means burning the Balzano family to ash?"

"Oh, fuck yes," Viv said, fangs out and practically salivating.

Gia had eyes for Aurora and no one else. She waited, uncertainty creeping into her expression.

Aurora cupped Gia's cheek. "I'm with you one hundred percent. However long it takes. Whatever we need to do. "

"But you don't even know why?"

"I know it'll be a damn good reason. Hell, taking your memories, making you sick, gaslighting you, and keeping you tied to them is reason enough."

"Agreed," Edward said, surprising Aurora this time.

Enacting vengeance wasn't the Lockwood Coven's way, as far as she'd known, but if the coven elders had been trying to free Gia for years, they'd want to see this through to the end.

Gia nodded, a shudder coursing through her as she gathered her words. "To gain power in Ashton Lakes, Franco killed the previous head of the mob and all his supporters, but it turns out, he didn't kill them with guns or men like Salvator. He had me do it."

Aurora reared back. "You?"

"With my magic. Once he realized Jeffrey was a witch and had passed his power on to me, he found a way to use me, though it took him five years to do it. He became a vampire when I was ten. There was some guy in the shadows, coaching him. I think he was a vampire, too. Franco would hypnotize me. Direct me to...to torture and kill his enemies, track their where-abouts, terrorize them until they came running to him for help against *unknown evil*."

"When you were ten?" Aurora's burning soul wavered. Her heart didn't need to be present for it to break.

"Why wait for me to grow up?" Gia laughed bitterly. "Franco wanted to seize power, and once he had it, he wanted more. Which meant keeping me dependent on him so I wouldn't leave. The only reason he didn't hypnotize me twenty-four-seven and keep me locked away was his image. I couldn't disappear from the public eye without drawing unwanted attention."

"Did everyone around you know?" Aurora was afraid of the answer. She wanted Gia to have had someone, *anyone*. But she had a feeling they were all complicit, and not in the way Gia feared she'd been over the years.

Gia nodded grimly. "They all knew. Franco hypnotized his men to keep my magic hidden from the outside world. It created an aura of power around him. The kind of fear that kept any rival humans from crossing him because they knew Franco never lost."

"He's going to fight like hell to take control of you again," Viv said in warning.

"Then we shouldn't wait to make our move," Aurora said. "We can't give Franco any more time to prepare."

Gia gave a decisive nod. "Agreed. Salvator knows I'm finally aware of magic. They won't need to pretend, and I doubt they'll approach me unprepared again."

"If they've found you already, let's lay a trap," Viv suggested. "Lure them to you and attack. One vampire and a bunch of humans will be easy prey."

"I wouldn't say easy." Aurora wanted to jump up and go as much as the vampire seemed to—for different reasons—but Franco's men weren't a bunch of humans. They were killers, and no one in the room was trained to fight.

Except Gia.

"Easy enough," Viv argued, reminding Aurora she had no idea who this lady was.

Gia shook her head. "I'm not so sure. Before I fled, Franco was looking for more powerful witches than his Ashton Lakes allies. It was all part of his plan to expand his empire. Before, I'd thought all his talk of expansion was about the drug and weapons trade. That's all he'd let me remember, but after what I just saw, I think it's something else. He wants more powerful allies in the magic world. He wants to expand beyond human crime."

Edward leaned forward in his seat. "Do you know if he found any new allies?"

"I'm not sure. He talked about the West Coast once or twice, but nothing specific in front of me. What if he was looking this way because it's where Jeffrey came from?"

Viv raised a brow. "You think he wanted to get rid of Jeffrey's surviving family?"

"Perhaps. Franco doesn't like loose ends. I'm surprised he didn't hunt Susan down years ago."

"Susan died of natural causes, right?" Aurora had heard as much, but it was worth checking.

"Yes, there's no disputing her cause of death." Edward ran a hand through his hair. "Most covens won't be interested in allying with a vampire who heads human organized crime, regardless of what he's planning. Franco might not have had any luck, even looking as broadly as the whole coast. I'll ask around and see if anything suspicious pops up. Until I hear, we should hold off tracking Franco down, in case he has new magical allies."

"How long will that take?" Aurora was uneasy. Getting information on the entire region's coven's alliances sounded like a huge undertaking. Especially when the Lockwoods didn't associate with the kind of witches Franco was likely to approach.

But making a move without a clear picture of what they were facing could get them all killed.

"I can get a solid answer in a day by calling in some favors. If Franco doesn't have a new coven working with him out here, we'll strike immediately. Before he has time to do anything else."

Viv's eyes gleamed, nearly glowing. "And what move are we aiming for? Fire? Beheading? Ripping out the wretch's heart? Those are your options for killing a vampire, in case you didn't know, Gia."

Gia didn't flinch at Viv's violent musings. Aurora was sure she would have yesterday. The fact that had changed because of what Franco had done made Aurora want to destroy the world and start over.

Gia nodded, but she seemed deep in thought. She reached for Aurora. "I think we should retrieve your body first."

"What?"

Gia ran her fingers along Aurora's forearm. "You need to be safe before we do this, and have access to your magic."

It would be best to have her full strength and ability. "But what if you need me to channel you? It could be our surprise move."

"I'm not completely clueless about magic anymore." A haunted look passed over Gia's face. "I know all kinds of horrible spells. I'm a weapon, and maybe I shouldn't want to use what Franco taught me, but turning it on him is the least of what he deserves."

Aurora's chest ached. "The very least. Do you know how to counter spells?"

Gia frowned. "No. I never went up against anyone with magic, which is why it'll be better to have you with me. At my side as a witch. You won't need to channel me like you did with Salvator if you have your magic."

"She has a point," Edward cut in. "If you're willing to fight with us—"

"Of course I'm willing."

Aurora wanted to be sure of what they'd find at the Thornfield compound before going for her body, but she had to admit they might not get any more information than Lilly had already uncovered. Not without infiltrating the compound to see what was happening, and the change in Gia's situation added an urgency that hadn't been there before.

Gia was right. Aurora needed her body and full power before facing Franco.

"If we go onto the Thornfield compound, we have to be ready for them to expect us."

Edward nodded. "I can send a diversion to distract them while you break past their wards."

Nerves churned in Aurora's soul. "Would anyone in the coven be willing to help break in? Unless...Gia, do you know how to break wards?"

"I don't." Gia might know plenty of ways to kill, but her magical knowledge was limited. Aurora would offer to channel her to break in, but she'd never broken a ward without detection, and they couldn't have her family running to meet them at the border.

"That's not a problem. I can break in for you," Viv said, sunny as a fucking daisy. "I love slipping past protective spells."

Aurora stared at her. "How? You're a vampire." She'd be excellent backup in a fight, but useless against warding spells. Other than hypnosis, vampires couldn't do any sort of magic.

Viv scowled. "Yes, we've established I'm a vampire. That doesn't mean I don't have a few tricks up my sleeve. My past has been colorful, shall we say."

Edward raised an eyebrow.

"Which we'll discuss another time," Viv said to him. She jabbed a thumb at Aurora and Gia. "Surely you'll consider accepting my application if I help these two?"

TWENTY-ONE

GIA

GIA SHOVED her newly uncovered memories into the depths of her mind, determined to concentrate on helping Aurora. Even if it would never undo the horrific things she'd witnessed—no, things she'd *done*—she could accomplish something good. Something she wanted to do, not was forced to.

"Are we in the right spot?" Viv asked Aurora, disconcertingly cheerful to be on her way to break into the Thornfield's property.

"This is the closest the road comes out here," Aurora confirmed.

Viv had driven Gia and Aurora out of the city in a beat-up old car that smelled like herbs, kind of like Sam's car had. When Gia had asked, Viv explained it was basic anti-tracking. Not foolproof, but better than nothing.

Why Viv had her car equipped with anti-tracking magic, Gia couldn't say. Surely she wasn't on the run, too.

They pulled over on the side of a narrow, unpaved road deep in the forest north of Shearwater Landing. It was surprising how quickly the trees sprang up once they'd passed through the suburbs.

Viv twisted around in the driver's seat. "You two wait here." She bounded out of the car and circled around to the trunk.

"Maybe it's knowing she's a vampire, but Viv's not what I expected," Gia whispered.

Aurora hummed in agreement. "Vampires are a different breed. She'll be good backup."

Gia's heart skipped. "Why do you sound worried?"

"Waiting in the hopes we can figure out if my family actually believes I died isn't worth it anymore. Not when we have Franco to face. But it occurred to me...the Nightingales could be here."

Gia clenched a fist. "You mean the guy you were supposed to marry?"

"Him, or his father. Other members of their coven. I wonder what happened to the alliance."

"Surely it's been called off, and the Nightingales aren't around."

Aurora shook her head. "My uncle was set on his plans to gain power. He'll find another in with the Nightingales. I'm sure of it. In case they already worked it out, a vampire's superhuman speed and near-indestructibility will come in handy."

"It sure will." Viv appeared at Gia's window, making her jump. "But let's not get caught. Mmkay?" She checked her phone. "Edward says the diversion is in place. Ready to go?"

The lawyer had sent several Lockwood Coven members to the section of forest nearest the main entrance, where there was a hiking trail and a park. The plan was for the witches to perform some innocuous rituals while foraging for herbs in order to snag the coven's attention.

Aurora was certain her family would detect and investigate any magic close to the property, even if it posed no threat. Everyone agreed it wasn't a good idea for too many people to break in, since they were going for stealth, not a fight, and with a handful of Lockwoods in the woods on the other side of the compound, it would be the perfect misdirection.

Gia climbed out of the car, followed by Aurora, who floated ahead, leading the way toward the compound's northernmost boundary.

As they quietly picked their way through the trees, Gia's skin prickled. She tried to stay in the moment. Concentrate on the plan. On Aurora. On the strange vampire. But her thoughts kept wandering down another path.

Horrific memories slithered through her mind, like she'd stepped into a waking dream. A nightmare. She did her best not to let the feelings register, reminding herself to look at it all later. She could fall apart once this was done. But even if she ignored all the gory details—the guilt—she couldn't pretend she was the same person who'd woken in bed next to Aurora that morning.

God, had it been only this morning?

The Gia from earlier today had never hurt anyone, didn't know how to cast a single spell, and had spent much of her life believing she was helpless. The woman she was now—had always been—was capable of making hardened criminals tremble without a care.

Detachment had been another of Franco's commands. Not simply to be quiet and not cry, but to not feel. Even if she'd had no choice, the memory of standing impassive—being a person without emotion—had become a part of Gia. It was like two people had merged. The old Gia and this hidden *thing*.

What would she do with this new monster inside her? She could say it wasn't her. Casting those spells had not been her choice. But the memories were hers. The capability was hers.

Yesterday, Gia would have said she'd never kill Franco. Now, she wasn't sure. She'd still never kill for power. For her own gain. Not for any of the reasons Franco killed. But to protect herself? To protect Aurora? It'd be much easier to take that step now than it would have been before.

Gia wasn't sure what to make of that change.

She called on her magic for the first time of her own free will and explored the depths of power within her. It was easier than she'd thought, but then, she'd done it countless times, hadn't she?

Familiar magic awakened within, and her stomach twisted in anticipation of something terrible. No. Nothing bad was happening. She was safe in the woods with Aurora and Viv. She had control.

All the things she'd done with her magic had been horrid, but it had been terrible to have no choice. One of the most terrible things, perhaps, and nothing like that would happen now. No deadly spells would twist her magic unless she decided.

What would she decide?

As Gia stepped through the trees, she was confident she'd be able to make peace with all her own decisions, but the things she'd done while under Franco's control were for *him* to make peace with, and enacting bloody vengeance on him would be deserved.

Aurora's ghostly form flickered ahead, and Gia let her tense muscles relax. Aurora understood her. Had stood by her. And now, Gia could use everything she'd learned to help her. Letting the Thornfields have a hold over her for even a moment longer wasn't an option. Gia wasn't afraid to take risks like she had been. She was ready to do what needed to be done.

She searched their surroundings for spells. Up ahead lay a hugely complex tangle of magic, and she stopped in her tracks, stunned she'd detected it so easily.

Aurora halted beside her, pointing toward the mess of magic. "The boundary starts right about there. I can't feel it, but

I'd recognize the edge of the property anywhere along the border."

How many times had she walked to the edge, unable to go further? Gia shivered.

"Perfect." Viv knelt and set a small wooden box she'd been carrying on the ground.

Aurora glanced sidelong at Gia. "That's how we're breaking in?"

"It is." Viv flicked the box open and stepped away.

There was a flash of light as what looked like dust erupted from the box. Particles billowed through the air, gradually coming to rest and forming a small translucent wall before them. No, not a wall. It was more like the shape of a door.

With another flash, the dust disappeared, leaving nothing behind. How anticlimactic.

Gia squinted, and a glimmer caught in the late afternoon light. An outline of a door remained, hardly visible. Gia brushed it with her magic but couldn't sense any power within the outline, even though the rest of the boundary remained unchanged.

She took a step closer. "There's a hole in the ward."

"Really?" Aurora swung to face Viv. "Where the hell did you get a trinket like that?"

Viv shrugged and sauntered through the magic door. "If I told you, I'd have to kill you."

Uncertainty washed over Gia. "Are you serious?"

"It's a good thing you don't have to find out," Viv called over her shoulder from the other side of the broken ward. "Hurry up. We have four hours before the spell wears off and the door closes."

Aurora floated after the vampire, quickly taking the lead, and Gia hurried to keep up. According to Aurora, they'd entered as far from the main buildings as possible, and weren't likely to encounter anyone unless they were particularly unlucky.

At a gap in the trees, Aurora paused, and Gia stopped beside her.

"The cemetery is this way." Aurora pointed ahead. "And the main house and outbuildings are that way." She pointed to where the forest grew thinner.

They'd agreed for Gia and Aurora to go straight to the crypt while Viv investigated the rest of the compound. In the event Aurora wasn't in the crypt, they'd reassess from there.

Viv came up behind them, disconcertingly silent on her feet. "I'll go see what I can find. Anyone headed your way won't make it."

Gia didn't ask exactly what Viv meant, and neither did Aurora. "Should we come find you when we're done?"

"No. You're too loud, crashing around." Viv rolled her eyes. "I'll meet you at the cemetery in twenty minutes. You shouldn't need longer to open a crypt."

Aurora flickered in and out of focus. "Fingers crossed."

Viv strode off without another word, like this was all perfectly normal. Even to Gia, it wasn't as strange as it should have been, as it *would* have been if her life hadn't turned upside down.

"How are you doing?" Aurora asked, voice painfully soft, almost as if she'd read Gia's mind.

"How am I doing? How are *you* doing? This is what you've been waiting for."

Aurora waved a hand. "I'm fine. Retrieving my body was always the plan." She floated in the direction of the cemetery.

Gia followed. "Being here isn't hard?"

Aurora's expression darkened. "No harder than it was any other day in my life. I'm ready to leave this place, these people, and never come back. I'd much rather help you figure out what you want to do next." She paused. "If you want me to, that is."

A smile tugged on Gia's lips. "Of course I want you. I think I've wanted that since I met you."

Aurora glowed brighter, her expression filling with determination. "We'll—" She disappeared.

Gia froze, her heart pounding, and every one of her senses on alert. "Aurora? Are you invisible?"

There was no answer.

"Aurora!" Gia spun around, searching the surrounding trees.

Not a flicker caught her eye. The cemetery was visible up ahead, a low stone wall at the edge of the trees and several looming crypts beyond. Were they close enough for Aurora to be called to her body? She'd been called to the theater when she hadn't wanted to go. Was the reverse happening now?

They should have done a better job of figuring out what tied the two of them together and what caused Aurora's soul to move from one place to another. Fuck! Gia had assumed nothing would separate them until they found Aurora's body.

"Aurora!" Gia screamed, her pulse pounding. She immediately clamped her mouth shut. What if one of the Thornfields heard her?

Gia ran toward the cemetery. Her feet tangled beneath her, and she fell with a crash, only just catching herself from face-planting.

"Goddammit." She'd tripped on uneven ground.

Gia pushed up on scraped palms. The dirt beneath her seemed loose compared to the rest of the compact ground around it, and was slightly raised. Like a mound.

Like someone had been digging and then filled in the hole.

A violent shiver vibrated through Gia's body. Her fists clenched in the loose dirt. This looked like a fresh grave. It was long enough, and about the right shape. But she was outside the cemetery, and there was no marker. Not even a stone or a single flower.

A muffled shout cut through the quiet woods.

Gia sat up like lightning. Was Viv yelling? No, she was too calm and collected. It almost sounded…

Gia looked at the disturbed earth, and everything went icy-cold.

"Oh, god. *Aurora?*" Was she down there?

Gia scraped frantically at the earth. What if the Thorn-fields believed Aurora had died but hadn't put her to rest in the crypt? Being buried outside a cemetery brought to mind old traditions, how churches excluded some people from hallowed ground.

Did witches have similar customs?

"Aurora!" Gia screamed, and her throat threatened to close around the pained sound. Fuck. Fuck. Fuck. Her hands were a blur as she dug in the dirt. "I'm coming! Please!"

A faint sound replied, almost too muffled to hear. Was that Aurora? Was Gia imagining things? There was no time to think. No way to be sure. How long could a person live buried under-ground before they suffocated?

If Aurora was in her body, she could die.

Gia's nails broke as she forced her hands deeper into the earth, clawing faster and faster, heaving sobs tearing from her throat. It wasn't enough. How deep was the grave? Gia swal-lowed a scream of agony.

Out of all the things she'd seen, this would be what broke her. She could take anything Franco had done, but not this. Not losing Aurora.

Magic! Gia had magic. Her motions slowed a fraction, but she couldn't stop digging. Did she know any spells that would help? Could she use magic to find out if Aurora was buried?

She sent her magic forth, probing the earth and hoping to find nothing but proof she was losing her mind.

A flicker responded.

There was someone with magic under there. And detectable power meant they were alive.

A scream tore out of Gia, her throat burning. She could hardly hear her own voice over the blood rushing in her ears. Her bleeding fingers turned numb as she clawed at the dirt, feeling nothing but a hollow, sinking dread.

She directed her power into the earth, letting it burst from her. The ground vibrated, loosening the soil, she released her magic again and again, throwing gobs of dirt to the side, but it wasn't enough.

Gia gathered her power and slashed her hand violently through the air as she'd done countless times before, sending men flying at Franco's command, and the earth opened, rocks and dirt exploding into the air. A nearby tree cracked.

It still wasn't enough. The hole she'd gouged from the earth wasn't deep enough. Gia did it again, cutting farther into the ground, scooping loose dirt out of the way as fast as she could.

She readied a third hit, and the ground vibrated. Gia hadn't done that. She froze, and Aurora's muffled scream shook her to her core.

TWENTY-TWO
AURORA

Aurora's whole body shivered, every bit of her cold and stiff. *I'm in my body.* There was no mistaking the weight of her flesh and bones. The cool air on her skin.

One second, she'd been with Gia, and the next, everything was black. Why was it so dark? Were her eyes even open?

Yes, they were. She must be in the crypt.

Being drawn into her body was unexpected. She'd assumed she'd have to float into herself once Gia got her body out in the open.

Another shiver raced through her. She'd think about the details later. It was damp in here, the air stale.

Why wasn't she covered with a shroud? Had they put her in the stone burial chamber without one?

She reached in front of her, unable to see her hand, and felt for the edges of the space. Instead of being met with stone, her fingers brushed wood.

What? Where was she?

Aurora's hands moved frantically, feeling all around. Rough wood surrounded her on all sides. This wasn't the crypt.

She was in a box. A wooden box that smelled of earth and must.

"No. I can't be." Was she *underground?*

Had she been buried?

A scream tore from Aurora's throat. She thrashed, banging her elbows and knees against wood. She had to get out. She had to escape.

The space closed in. She would run out of air and die. After everything, she'd die and lose her chance at having the life she wanted.

Aurora didn't want to die. She never had. All she'd ever wanted was to escape, and now she never would.

Her eyes were wet, her throat burning, but Aurora forced herself to still, to stop screaming, stop using up her limited air. She had to think. She couldn't bust her way out, not if she was underground—the thought nearly had her screaming once more —but no. She could figure this out.

Could she suspend her body again? Repeating her initial spell might mean she'd be pulled to Gia's side. Or even the theater. Anywhere was better than here.

Would the spell work without the power of flame?

She had to try. Closing her eyes against the oppressive darkness, Aurora called on her magic and scrambled desperately to catch hold of it. *Damnation.* She could get it together and fucking do this. She had to. She wasn't dying today.

Magic swelled inside her, and she seized it. The spell was complex, and her concentration and willpower were shot to Hell, but still, she pushed through.

Nothing happened. Her soul remained in her damned body.

A scream bubbled from the depths of Aurora's chest, her ears popped, and every one of her muscles shook.

The faint sound of an answering scream tickled the edge of her hearing, and she stilled. *Oh Satan, is that Gia?*

The earth vibrated around Aurora, and she gasped, her arms flying out to catch herself. She heaved a breath, yet hardly any air seemed to enter her lungs. How much time did she have left before she suffocated? Would Gia reach her in time?

The earth vibrated again. And again.

Aurora couldn't do this. Her breathing shallowed, chest clenching so tight her lungs burned.

With a scream, Aurora unleashed her magic, and power exploded out of her. She prayed she wouldn't be crushed to death when the coffin broke, but she needed it to break. It was the only way out. Her magic would have to be enough to blast her way to the surface.

Wood cracked and splintered, everything around her shaking, but nothing changed. Nothing but blackness greeted her teary gaze, and when she pushed on the wood inches above her face, it didn't budge.

Aurora swallowed her next scream and released another blast.

The coffin shattered. Thank the Devil, it seemed to be cheap wood rather than anything sturdy. Aurora released more magic and pushed upward to carve her way out. At last, her hands broke through cracked wood and sent soil pouring onto her face. She scrambled, tearing her hands through the dirt, her magic working to keep the earth from pulling her under.

She would not be crushed. Not by this. Not after the life she'd lived. Aurora surged upward along with her magic, but she was still underground, dirt all around.

How far was the surface?

There was no air left. She struggled, panic shredding her insides, the urge to breathe overwhelming, dirt on her face and pushing against her closed lips.

A vibration from above met Aurora's frantic blasts of magic, and the crushing pressure eased.

"Aurora! I'm coming!" Gia's voice rained down on her, sweeter than any sound she'd ever heard.

Aurora struggled harder, and her hand broke free, warm air enveloping her skin in a burning contrast to the cold soil crushing her body. Fingers wrapped around her wrist and pulled, another hand digging into the dirt along her arm until it met her neck.

Gia clasped Aurora's nape in an iron grip and heaved, lifting her out of the earth.

Aurora gasped, the sound of her desperate breath rattling the air. Her lungs burned as she sucked air in.

"Oh my god, Aurora!" Gia cried as frantic hands wiped dirt from Aurora's cheeks. "I've got you. I've got you. Oh god."

Gia wrapped her arm around Aurora and pulled her farther out of the grave. Aurora tasted soil on her lips. Her vision blurred with renewed tears, mingling with the dirt in her eyes and on every inch of her skin.

"Gia," she sputtered. "You saved me."

Gia stilled, then pulled away to meet Aurora's eyes, her face splotchy red and expression wild. She was as covered in dirt as Aurora, and it was the most transcendent thing Aurora had ever seen.

Heart racing, Aurora tangled a bloody and soil-stained hand in Gia's messy hair and tugged her into a kiss, their mouths meeting in a desperate crash. Gia gasped, body stiff, then melted into Aurora, arms tightening around her.

Aurora groaned, almost a growl, and deepened the kiss, chasing the sweet taste of Gia. Their tongues tangled, mixing the bitterness of salty tears and soil. Aurora realized she was crying again and didn't care. Hot tears had never felt so good.

Summer air had never been so refreshing. Another body had never been this comforting against her.

For a second, Aurora swore she was floating. If Gia's grip hadn't been so tight, she'd have feared she'd vacated her body. But Gia grounded her, and Aurora never wanted to be anywhere else.

Gasping for breath was no longer terrifying. It meant she and Gia were one, consumed by each other, and Aurora chased the feeling. This kiss was life. It could devour her whole, and she'd never be happier.

Without breaking the kiss, Aurora crawled the rest of the way from her grave, flattening Gia on her back in the piles of dirt, and straddled her hips. Gia moaned, one hand finding its way to Aurora's ass, the other in her hair.

Aurora couldn't get enough. Her core tightened, and she rolled her hips, arousal spiking at Gia's responding whimper.

She'd fuck Gia, right here. Make Gia hers, like it was the only thing that mattered in life. Because it was.

"Aurora," Gia moaned against her lips. "I thought I lost you, and I can't… I need you. Don't stop."

Aurora nipped Gia's bottom lip. "I need you too."

She didn't mean Gia's body, though she desired every inch of her. She needed Gia's love and the opportunity to love her in return. Needed the two of them together from now on, so these feelings could blossom into something deeper. Because they would. The clarity of the realization would have shocked her if it hadn't been so wonderful.

"I like a show as much as the next girl, but we need to get the fuck out of here."

Aurora and Gia froze.

Viv stood over them, her hands on her hips. "Heard you screaming like a banshee, Gia. Not exactly subtle. Get moving."

Aurora scrambled off Gia and held out a hand to pull her to her feet. "Are the Thornfields headed this way?"

"Not yet, but even without vampire hearing, I doubt anyone missed the scream fest."

Gia glared at Viv. "Aurora was trapped in a *grave*. Underground."

"I see." Viv wrinkled her nose at the mess of upturned earth. "Let's get the fuck going." She marched off in the direction of the car.

Aurora grabbed Gia's hand and pulled her after the vampire.

Poor Gia looked stricken. "I shouldn't have been so loud."

Aurora huffed. "No one but an immortal could have kept their head in this situation. Don't worry about it. I don't hear anyone coming yet."

They picked up the pace, running through the trees until the magic door appeared up ahead.

Viv was already unlocking the car. "Grab the box when you're through, will you?"

Gia stepped through the strange door, pulling Aurora after her. A sharp pain shot up Aurora's arm, and she wrenched her hand from Gia's.

Gia flexed her fingers. "Ow! What was that?"

All of Aurora's giddy joy fled, leaving her empty. She was still on the other side of the boundary. Inside the compound's grounds. She tried to step closer to Gia and couldn't get her feet to move.

"Hurry up!" Viv yelled.

Gia's brow furrowed. "Aurora, what's wrong?"

She swallowed, her throat dry. "I can't get out. It didn't work. My whole plan. The spell. Leaving my body didn't sever my ties."

Gia's expression was ashen. "What?"

Aurora fisted her hands in her hair. "I can't get off the property. I'm still tied here. Still bound."

Oh Satan, she should have realized. Not all of her magic had escaped when she'd been a ghost. Her inability to cast spells meant the magic in her blood had remained in her body and had never been free. The link that bound her had remained untouched.

She'd been right that nothing could contain a pure soul, but freeing that soul didn't sever the rest as she'd hoped. Not while she remained alive.

"I'm still bound," she repeated, frantic.

Gia stepped through the magic door, seemingly without a second thought, and clasped Aurora's hand. "We'll find another way to free you."

Tears welled in Aurora's eyes. "How? The only other way is to break the binding, and I can't cast spells against my family. I'm right back where I started."

"No." Gia squeezed her hand, expression hardening into something more determined than Aurora had ever seen. "You are not back where you started. I'm here with you. I'll break you free."

Aurora's heart skipped. "You don't know the right spells. You said you've never had to counter anything. Breaking a binding like this isn't easy."

"It doesn't have to be easy. Tell me what to do. What spells to cast. We'll break it right now."

A tear fell down Aurora's cheek. "Some spells need more than words and access to power. We need my uncle's blood to undo the binding because blood is how he created it. I can't break free without facing him, and even then, it's not as simple as reciting a known spell."

"Okay, so we'll face him. And if it's more complicated than

having me repeat a spell, channel me. Isn't there a way for you to control my magic, like we did before?"

"I can't *use* you." Not after everything Franco had done.

"Why not?" Gia closed the remaining distance between them. "I'm giving you permission. I have unrestricted power, and you have the knowledge to undo the binding. We can do this together."

Satandammit, Gia was serious. She'd pulled Aurora out of her grave, and as if it weren't enough, she offered up her essence like it was the most natural thing. Aurora's knees went weak, and her heart swelled, the sturdy beat giving her strength. "Witches can channel each other, but it's blood magic that most people never mess with."

"Why not?"

"Channeling gives another witch access to *all* your power. It's the riskiest kind of blood magic. You could easily drain someone to death." The only saving grace was that, unlike other practices, like leeching, it was impossible to channel against someone's will.

Gia didn't seem deterred by the warning. "What's the alternative? Leave you here until we can get the Lockwoods to come and fight for you? Will they know how to unbind you?"

"I'm not sure."

The Lockwoods didn't know how the binding was created. And even if they did, how many people could she ask to fight for her? Especially those who weren't fighters. There was a whole host of reasons she'd never planned to ask the Lockwoods to rescue her by force.

"Then tell me what to do. Channel me." Gia squeezed Aurora's clammy fingers once more. "I trust you with my magic."

Aurora's heart clenched. "We have to exchange blood with the intention to share power. You're super powerful, by the way.

Did I tell you? Way more powerful than me, so you should have no trouble casting spells while I channel you, as long as you don't start to feel strained. If you do, you have to stop."

Gia nodded. "Okay. I know what you mean. Sometimes, after Franco...I'd feel spent, my magic almost thin."

The bastard had pushed Gia to her limits? Aurora fumed. She could not wait to get her hands on the damned mobster, but she needed to focus.

"Good. You'll know when to stop, and so will I. But this won't be like when I channeled you before. You won't move as I do, or say the words I say. It will look like the magic is coming from me, while you sense me taking your power."

"Perfect." Gia grinned, a feral glint in her eye. "They won't see it coming."

A thrill shot through Aurora. No, they wouldn't. How long had she wanted to strike back? And here Gia was, giving her that gift.

But one last thread of caution nagged at her. There was no getting around how risky this plan was. Could Aurora take on her uncle? She wasn't sure of the depth of his power. He'd no doubt become complacent, too used to oppressing his enemies, but would it be enough of an advantage?

Viv had crept closer as they'd talked and stepped through the magic door, saying, "In case it wasn't clear, I'm in."

Damnation, this was really happening. Aurora swore she could taste freedom, and it shared all the same sweet notes as Gia's lips.

"I appreciate it, Viv. What did you see when you went spying earlier?"

She waved a hand. "Not much. A few witches and a human in the yard, movement in the big house—"

"A human?" Aurora interrupted.

Viv nodded. "He was talking with a younger witch."

But the Thornfields didn't work with humans. "Maybe the Nightingales are here after all, and they brought someone." Although Aurora would have sworn they were as anti-human as her uncle.

"Whatever." Viv rolled her eyes. "Humans don't matter. How are we getting to your uncle? Any guesses where he might be?"

"He could be anywhere on the compound."

"Wait." Gia tugged on Aurora. "You weren't in the crypt. Does that mean your family believes you died or not? If we find your uncle without being detected, maybe we can take him by surprise before he has a chance to fight."

Aurora led Gia and Viv toward the main buildings as she considered. "They could have put me in the ground outside the cemetery for disgracing them by killing myself, rather than doing my duty. Meaning yeah, they believed I died."

Gia made a savage growling sound. "They're fucking horrible. No compassion, even when they thought you took your own life."

"I know, babe. But the other option is worse."

Gia's steps faltered. "What do you mean?"

Aurora clutched Gia tight. "They might have buried me, knowing my soul would reenter my body, and I'd die trapped underground, unable to get out."

The color drained from Gia's dirt-smeared face.

"Either way, they aren't expecting you," Viv said, all business and no emotion.

Aurora nodded to the vampire, glad to brush past the horror of what might have happened. Dwelling wouldn't do any good right now.

"I'll stay out of sight. Silent backup." Viv zipped into the trees and disappeared.

"Ready?" Aurora asked.

"Let's do this." Gia gripped both Aurora's hands in hers and sank her teeth into her lower lip, worrying at the flesh until it bloomed red with blood.

Aurora leaned in on reflex and licked the drops from Gia's plush lip, dipping her tongue inside her mouth for good measure. Gia hummed, sucking Aurora's lip into her mouth, then bit her hard, tantalizingly sucking her flesh. Aurora's stomach tightened.

Gia pulled away, breathless. "You can have all my power. Let me do this for you. There's nothing I want more."

Aurora kissed her, putting all her feelings into each brush of their lips. "Together then."

TWENTY-THREE
AURORA

THey picked their way through the forest, giving the cemetery a wide berth. Aurora paused. A faint voice carried through the trees, but she couldn't make out who it was. As she debated detouring to investigate, everything went silent.

A scream cut through the air, then cut off. Seemed Viv worked fast.

"What if that was your uncle?" Gia whispered as they reached the first of the outbuildings.

"He wouldn't creep around the woods himself." Aurora ushered Gia past a shed on the edge of the forest, and the main house came into view on the opposite side of the field. "What's the point of having underlings if you don't send them to do everything for you?"

"True. Franco would have done the same. It's creepy how similar they—" Gia gasped, her eyes going wide as she froze in place.

"Gia!" Aurora caught her as she fell, her body a heavy, dead weight in Aurora's arms.

The crunch of leaves underfoot sent Aurora's heart thundering. Someone was behind her. Aurora checked Gia's pulse, finding it slow but strong beneath her fingers. It must have been a stunning spell.

Was there time to cast a counter spell? Aurora turned toward the approaching footsteps, and her mother stepped out from behind the shed.

"Aurora." Virginia betrayed no hint of surprise. Shouldn't the sight of her daughter, fresh out of her grave, evoke some emotion other than cold fury, even if she'd been watching and had time to school herself?

Aurora's throat ran dry. With Gia unconscious, she couldn't channel her magic. When Aurora had been a ghost, the usual rules of magic didn't always apply. Like being invisible. There was a chance she'd have been able to join with Gia as a ghost and work through her, even if she were out of it. That wouldn't work now. Channeling between witches needed continuous consent on both sides.

She was as defenseless as she'd ever been, and worse, she couldn't protect Gia.

"I don't know how she got past our wards." Virginia gestured carelessly at Gia. "But it doesn't matter now. You won't be leaving with her, so why not come with me? Stan needs to see you urgently."

Aurora's grip on Gia tightened. "That's all you have to say after I crawled out of a coffin? Stan needs to see me urgently?"

"If you didn't want to be put to rest, you shouldn't have abandoned your body in such a lifeless—or should I say soulless?—position. Do you have any idea what you've cost us? All Stan's plans are ruined."

Damn it, where's Viv when you need her? Aurora didn't have the energy for her mother's bullshit.

"Leave the trespasser where she belongs." Virginia's voice rose, and she swept out a commanding arm, sending magic cutting through the air.

Power hit Aurora in the chest, and she staggered to the side, dropping Gia.

"Come with me." Her mother pointed toward the main house. "Don't make me force you."

Aurora bit the inside of her cheek until she tasted blood. She walked as slowly as possible, but didn't try to resist. The last thing she needed was her mother hurting Gia more than she already had.

What else could Aurora do? She saw no way out of this.

The back door to the house opened, and three familiar men strode across the lawn. Her uncle's steps faltered, his pale face losing color at the sight of her. Had he expected someone else? From what Virginia had said, they'd known she wasn't dead. Stan had expected her to suffocate, and here she was.

Sick satisfaction at catching him off guard coiled inside Aurora. She wouldn't be beaten down easily. But without Gia, Stan's momentary fear meant little. He still had power over her and seemed to remember as much.

Stan's surprise smoothed over. By the time he stood in front of Aurora, meeting halfway between the trees and the house, he wore his usual self-important sneer.

"Aurora, I thought we made it clear we no longer need you."

She flinched as if he'd slapped her, hating that he could still cause her pain. She didn't care what he thought. Didn't want anything from him, least of all to be of value to him. But still. He'd buried her in the ground, knowing she was alive and assuming she'd die.

"You expected me to suffocate?" She lifted her chin, pretending his cruelty was nothing to her. "Maybe you should have dug deeper."

"Perhaps you should have done as you were told and solidified our alliance with the Nightingales. As soon as I asked to postpone the betrothal, they dropped us faster than hot coal.

Claimed we were unreliable and not what they'd hoped. All because of you."

Aurora fumed, even though she was glad to hear the Nightingales weren't around. "Seems like pinning your alliance on me was a dumb idea. You can try as hard as you want, but you can't control me."

"No?" Stan cocked his head. "What are you still doing here then?"

Aurora swallowed a scream, the desire to escape swelling within her.

She glanced over her shoulder. Virginia stood over Gia, who remained slumped on the ground, and Viv was nowhere to be seen. Even if Aurora could escape, she couldn't run and leave Gia defenseless.

No matter how fiercely Aurora raged inside, she was defenseless too, a caged animal, and her keeper knew it.

Panic threatened the edges of Aurora's senses. She clenched a shaking fist, trying desperately to come up with a plan. Her next move. *Anything.* She reached inward, searching for...she didn't even know what.

Something responded. A tickle of warmth caressed the magic within her. Was it Gia's?

Hope tore through Aurora, and she reached for Gia's power. It pulsed stronger, like it was offering itself up, waiting and ready to give her everything it could.

Gia must have woken and had the forethought to remain limp. Satan bless that smart woman. Aurora wanted nothing more than to kiss her until her lips were raw.

Soon. She'd give Gia the world as soon as she got them out of this mess.

Aurora faced her uncle, a smile stretching her lips. "What am I still doing here? I came to find you."

His brow furrowed in confusion, and Aurora unleashed

Gia's power. Waving her arms, she sent magic barreling into Stan's advisors, sending them flying.

Stan staggered, horror breaking over his face. "What?"

Aurora didn't hesitate. She sent a stunning spell straight for his chest.

He got his shit together in time to block it, his beady eyes narrowing. "How?" he snarled.

Aurora wrapped a silencing spell around his throat. She'd heard more than enough from him.

Eyes bulging, Stan struck, hitting Aurora in the shoulder. She cried out at the pain and struck back, taking her uncle out at the knees.

Hands tangled in Aurora's hair from behind, and she lurched backward, stumbling into her mother's clutches. Stan got to his feet, his face red with fury.

Virginia muttered a counter-spell, freeing Stan's voice.

"Kill her," he rasped, clutching his throat.

Aurora felt her mother stiffen behind her. Was she hesitating? Even after leaving Aurora for dead underground?

The hands gripping Aurora's hair went slack, and her mother toppled to the side. Aurora managed to pull away and turned to see Gia rising from the ground, power glowing at her fingertips.

It wasn't hesitation or a change of heart. Virginia had been stunned.

Aurora and Gia's eyes locked, and the power flowing between them flared. Aurora faced her uncle, his advisors flanking him once more. She stunned the one on the left as blood bloomed across the chest of the one on the right. He screamed, clawing at his shirt in confusion.

That must have been Gia's doing.

Stan roared, striking Aurora with a blast of power. She was knocked on her ass, but all she did was laugh, hysteria bubbling inside her. She wasn't the real threat here, and Stan could do nothing to keep her incapacitated for long.

Not with Gia by her side.

Blood bloomed on Stan's chest, and he screamed. More cuts speared across his cheeks and arms, blood soaking his clothes. Howling, he dropped to his knees.

Gia held out a hand to help Aurora up. "How much of his blood do you need?"

"Not much." Aurora heaved to her feet.

Gia curled her fingers, and Stan was dragged forward by an invisible force until he slumped, whimpering at her feet. Aurora grabbed his bloody cheeks and covered her palms in his blood.

"That'll be enough," she told Gia, stunning Stan and tossing him aside. "Cover me?"

Gia nodded, moving in close, and Aurora knelt on the ground, digging her fingers into the grass. She searched for the binding linking the Thornfield Coven to this cursed earth, and when she found it, she sent Gia's considerable power into it, burning the blood binding from the inside out, picking apart each thread of the spell. The enforced hierarchy. The leader's control. The restriction on magic. The intricate knots keeping them prisoner.

Grass crisped beneath her fingers as she worked, checking for every possible link in the magic. The soil beneath Aurora grew hot. Heat radiated around her, fiercer than the summer sun. Her palms burned, and she had to fight to keep her hands in place, but she wouldn't let up until the binding was broken.

There was no stopping now.

Aurora bit her lip, vaguely aware of Gia blasting someone away. The dirt burned even hotter beneath her fingers, but she didn't let go. With a strangled cry, she sent one last jolt of Gia's power into the earth. Into the blood binding.

The blood coating her hands—her uncle's blood—turned to

flame, and fire shot from Aurora's palms out along the grass, flames roaring in the four cardinal directions as something seemed to snap deep within her.

Aurora jolted away from the flames. She cradled her hands, surprised to see them unharmed, clean of her uncle's blood, and free of burns.

Gia gripped her shoulder, hauling her upright. "Are you okay?"

"Fine." She gripped Aurora's elbow for support. "You?"

"All good. You haven't gotten close to draining my power." There was a wild look in Gia's eye, almost a sparkle. "Did it work?"

"I think so. Something snapped when I burned the last of the binding." Aurora didn't feel any different, but then the binding had never been something she sensed unless she actively struggled against it.

The flames cutting through the grass went out, but the fire had reached the trees and the shrubbery lining the house. Stan stirred in the grass beside them, recovering from the stunning spell and unharmed by the flames.

Aurora lashed out, this time with her power, not Gia's, and Stan was thrown into the air, landing near the house with a thud.

"It's gone." She stared at him in dazed wonder. "The binding is gone."

Gia grabbed her hand. "Thank god. We better get out of here. I don't know where Viv is."

Damn it. They'd have to find her.

A booming explosion rocked the earth, throwing them to the ground. *What the hell was that?* Aurora looked wildly around. There was nothing near the trees, but as her attention landed on the house, she froze.

The fire burning the bushes must have spread to the gas

canisters stored along the wall. There was nothing but a gaping hole in the building where they'd been.

Fire spread up the wall, and screams came from inside as people spilled out of every exit.

"Shit." Aurora hoped people hadn't been in the back of the massive house. Well, there were more than a few coven members that she wouldn't have cared had they been, but not every one of the Thornfields was like Stan.

There were other witches like her. Trapped and beaten down.

Another of Stan's top men ran from the building, searching frantically until he spotted his fallen leader. Two other men ran in Aurora's direction, pointing and shouting, their faces red with anger.

Gia's grip on her tightened. "We can't fight them all off. Not this many at once."

Aurora raised her arms, ready to strike. "We have to try. At least enough to escape."

Gia nodded, pulling Aurora toward the trees.

Two more men and a woman headed off the lackeys charging toward Aurora, and a fight broke out between the five of them. Another woman descended upon Stan, flashes of light filling the air as he fought against her attack. Not too far away, a woman near Aurora's age attacked one of Stan's junior advisors.

Other witches ran straight for the borders. More fights broke out, more people joining in the attack on Stan and his closest allies, until every upper member of the coven was outnumbered by the people they'd kept prisoner.

"Holy shit," Gia muttered.

Aurora felt dazed. No one was paying attention to her any longer. It was chaos. They should run, but Aurora was rooted to the spot.

Her gaze returned to Stan. He was nothing more than a bloody heap, torn apart by the people he'd abused.

She flinched away from the sight.

"Let's go." Gia wrapped an arm around Aurora, shielding her vision and pulling her away.

A bellowing scream tore through the air, and it sounded like more people were running out of the house as the fire spread.

Aurora and Gia had almost reached the trees when an unfamiliar voice called out.

"Stop right there!"

Gia stilled, a tremble running through her as her magic raged, sparking along its connection to Aurora. But Gia wasn't trembling in fear, Aurora realized with sudden clarity. She was seething.

Gia turned slowly, pushing Aurora behind her. "Franco, what the hell are you doing here?"

TWENTY-FOUR
GIA

GIA'S POWER THRUMMED, roiling in response to her shock. Where the hell had Franco come from? Had he followed her here?

A man Gia recognized ran from the burning building, pulling another along with him. "Everyone's out!" he shouted.

They'd been *in* the house?

Franco didn't acknowledge the man's words. All his attention was on Gia, his eyes glowing orange as they had in all the memories he'd erased.

Gia's pulse thudded, anger at what he'd done consuming her. "I was a child." The words tore from her in a snarl.

Franco sauntered closer, Salvator falling into step beside him. "But you aren't now."

So, he wasn't feigning ignorance over what she was talking about. It was all out in the open.

Gia's vision tunneled. Not even the growing flames consuming the house penetrated her focus. She saw nothing but Franco's glowing eyes.

Harnessing her power, she slashed a hand through the air.

Blood bloomed across Franco's face as a gash opened from his ear to his chin, splitting his lips.

He smiled a gruesome, lopsided smile as blood covered his teeth and steamed down his neck. His sickening laugh filled the air, and the bleeding slowed to a stop, his mouth knitting back together.

A chill wound through Gia.

Franco wiped his face with the cuff of his suit jacket. "I'm impressed, Gianna. Good for you. I never guessed you'd have such fight in you. Such willpower. Perhaps weakening you was a mistake."

"You're a bastard for making her sick along with everything else," Aurora shouted.

She grabbed Aurora's hand, holding her firmly in place. Franco wouldn't get his hands on her. She'd make sure of it.

Franco made a dismissive gesture. "We had to explain the memory loss somehow. But it doesn't have to be that way anymore. I see now that I may have"—his eyes narrowed—"miscalculated. Come home, Gia. Sit at my side. You are my fiercest enforcer, after all."

"Gia, please." Marc had joined them without her noticing. He took a step closer, and Franco held out a hand to stop him.

Gia's eyes stung, but she didn't let the pained look in Marc's face sway her. "How can you stand by him?"

Marc's posture straightened. "It's who we are, G. I had to be ready to take over—"

"Are you an idiot? Take over? Marc, he's a vampire. There will be no taking over. You'll grow old and die, and Franco will still be scheming away."

Marc's face paled. "*Vampire?*" He whirled on Franco. "You said it was magic. Vampires aren't real."

He didn't know the truth? Franco had lied to him, too?

Of course, he'd lied. Marc might not have gone along with

everything if he'd known he'd never inherit the kingdom. Wanting the empire for himself wasn't an excuse for all he'd watched Franco do. Even if Marc hadn't known everything, he'd known enough. Their mother's murder. Franco's control over Gia's power. He'd been present in more than a few of her erased memories.

"Marc, now is not the time," Franco snapped. Marc's face twisted in anger, but Franco didn't seem to notice. "What do you say, Gianna? Come home and take a place by my side. I should have given it to you when you turned eighteen. Let's make up for it."

Gia sent her magic cutting through the air and hit Franco in the chest, slicing through his suit to gouge into his chest. "You killed my mother. I'll never stand beside you."

Franco clenched a fist, and more men gathered around him. There were almost a dozen, including Marc and Salvator. All of them had been privy to Franco's manipulation, present in the nightmares he'd erased. But they were all human. Gia's magic confirmed it.

Humans weren't a problem. She could deal with them as she'd done many times before, and this time, she'd be striking against people who had hurt *her*, not Franco's enemies. All she needed to do was get close enough to rip out Franco's heart, and if anyone retaliated, she'd flay them open.

Franco's glowing eyes flared. "Look at me," he said at the same time as Aurora yelled, "Gia, look away!"

She tugged frantically on Gia's hand, but Gia's gaze was locked on Franco, and she couldn't pry it away.

Ice filled her veins.

"Step away from the young woman and come here," Franco commanded, his voice silky smooth.

Gia obeyed, dropping Aurora's hand, and approached Franco at an unhurried pace.

No! She barely kept the scream from passing her lips. Aurora might have been freed, but Gia was as much a prisoner as she'd always been. Franco could wipe all her newfound knowledge from her brain, take her home, and she'd never know any of this had happened.

Her magic thrashed inside her, and she could hardly think. She should have seen this coming, but Franco had appeared out of nowhere. She was supposed to have time to prepare for this confrontation, time to ask how to combat hypnosis.

She reached for Aurora. Not with a hand—she couldn't control her body—but with her magic.

Help.

Aurora's power responded, wrapping around Gia in a feeling more secure than anything she could remember.

"Call on your power and repeat after me." Franco sounded bored as he began the spell for an explosion.

Gia's heart skipped. Aurora was following too closely behind her. An explosive spell would kill her.

Gia's lips moved, and she was powerless to stop them. She longed to scream. To say anything other than the spell that would hurt the woman she was growing to love.

The last word of the spell tasted like acid, and Gia braced herself.

Nothing happened.

But she'd said the words. Why hadn't her magic responded? She'd called on it—she'd been forced to—but, she now realized, it hadn't come as requested.

"What the Devil?" Franco yelled, rushing forward and grabbing her arm. His eyes flared brighter. "Call on your magic and hand over control. Allow me to wield it. Speak as I speak. Act as if we are one."

Gia's head swam with the commands. She called on her power, but Aurora held it hostage. The tight squeeze was unmistakable now. It constricted, keeping her magic grounded. Keeping it from Franco.

She'd given Aurora permission to channel her, and it seemed her hold was more powerful than anything Franco could command.

"You can't have her." Aurora's voice was calm and threatening.

"*Witch*," Franco snarled, spit flying. "Salvator, kill her."

Before anyone could move, the men were blasted backward.

Gia wanted nothing more than to tear her gaze away from Franco's glowing eyes and see what Aurora was doing behind her, but she couldn't.

Franco growled and shook Gia violently. "Damn you! Why isn't this working?" He fixated on something behind her. "Look at me, witch."

"Make me, vamp," Aurora spat.

"Gia, stun her," he commanded.

The words passed Gia's lips, her arm reaching for Aurora as if it were someone else's, but her magic was locked down, and the spell came to nothing.

Franco roared, his fangs descending as his grip on her tightened past bruising to near bone-shattering.

"Let her go!" Aurora shouted. "Walk away, and maybe I won't kill you."

"Kill me?" Franco scoffed. "You can't kill me."

Aurora clutched the back of Gia's neck, her palm growing hot at the contact. "I can, and I will," she snarled. "Now, let Gia go."

Gia's magic surged, escaping Aurora's tight hold to flow through her once more. Had Aurora's concentration broken? Gia's heart thundered, sweat breaking out on her brow. She didn't want control of her magic. Aurora had to keep it safe.

Franco's hypnotic link to her flared, and her magic latched onto it. Franco's face twisted in pain, and he screamed.

Gia stared in shock.

"Let her go," Aurora commanded as she directed Gia's power, pushing it further into the link between Gia and Franco.

Franco inhaled through his nose, gritting his teeth against the pain. "Fuck you."

The smell of burning flesh met Gia's nose, and she recoiled. Was her magic doing that? Was Aurora using the connection created by his command to burn him like she'd burned the binding?

Yes. That's exactly what she was doing. Gia shook, nearly overwhelmed by her magic's ferocity. "Let me go, Franco, or my magic will burn you alive."

He snarled, his eyes flaring red. "Stop what you're doing," he commanded.

But Gia couldn't stop because she wasn't doing anything. Aurora was in charge, and Franco was giving her an easy path to destroying him by keeping her under his thrall.

"I said stop!" With an animalistic screech, Franco threw Gia to the side and lunged for Aurora, but her eyes were clamped shut to keep Franco's hypnosis at bay.

A gunshot went off. Someone screamed. Gia whirled around in time to see Viv tackling the man nearest them, his handgun flying across the grass.

Franco grabbed Aurora, and they fell to the ground as he tried to pry her eyelids open. She thrashed beneath him, screaming, but didn't release her hold on Gia's magic.

"Stop, Franco!" Gia yelled.

Marc appeared at her side. "Father, listen to her! Please."

Franco's skin began to smoke. He pushed Aurora away, staggered to his feet, and lunged for Gia instead.

"Kill her!" he roared, his breaths growing short. "Stop her."

This time, the words were nothing more than a gasp, and everyone around them looked aghast at Franco's fallibility.

The light in his eyes faded as Gia's magic burned him from the inside out and he slumped to the ground, unmoving.

This was the only death Gia wouldn't feel guilty about. She'd killed so many people for him, and even though she'd had no choice, she carried the pain of their deaths. She'd give anything to undo it. But this? This was earned. It was a fitting end for Franco Balzano and she was relieved it was over.

Salvator turned and ran, the others following without a backward glance.

"He's dead, right?" Gia asked.

"We might need to toss him in the actual fire," Aurora said in her ear, almost apologetic. When had she come so close? Her arm wrapped around Gia, and she gestured to the burning house. "I don't know if magic can burn thoroughly enough to prevent him from regenerating. His body is still intact, after all."

Viv appeared at their side. "Yeah, you're gonna need that extra step if you don't want him waking up."

"Where the fuck have you been?" Aurora asked her.

"Someone snapped my neck, and it took a hot minute to heal. *Sorry*." The last word dripped with sarcasm.

Aurora seemed mollified. "At least you're okay."

Viv shrugged and pointed at Franco. "What's the verdict with this one?"

"Toss him on the fire," Gia said, her voice oddly distant, even to herself.

Viv hummed agreeably. "Gotcha. Look away if you don't want to watch."

Gia didn't bother. Out of all the horrible things she'd seen, she needed this. She had to know it was over, so she watched as Viv threw Franco's body into the fire consuming the house.

The Thornfields seemed to have fled along with Franco's

men, except for the ones who'd been killed. Bodies littered the lawn, and fire burned in the distant trees. It was a hellscape. Only Marc remained, staring blankly at the burning building. At his father, Gia supposed.

Franco might not have been her birth father, but he had raised her, and now, he was gone. The price for what he'd done to Letti and Jeffrey was paid at last.

Exhaustion overwhelmed Gia. She was ready for the day to be done. To move on to something better.

"I'm worried about starting a wildfire," Aurora said as the flames raged.

Viv looked at her like she'd grown a second head. "Give Mr. Vamp a few more minutes to crisp, then we can put it out."

Aurora couldn't argue with that, but they might as well start with the trees.

A cursory investigation revealed that the fire was magically contained to the Thornfield compound, preventing it from spreading to the surrounding forest. Even though Aurora had destroyed the binding magic, the fire's link to the boundary spell must have kept it in check. While trees and buildings within the grounds turned to ash, nothing beyond the borders caught fire, so it seemed there was nothing to worry about.

The Lockwoods, who had been nearby creating the diversion, helped Aurora and Gia put out the flames, finally extinguishing the house once Viv deemed Franco properly destroyed.

As they'd hoped, a group of Thornfields had come to investigate what the Lockwoods were up to in the park, but when the fighting broke out, and they realized they were free, they wasted no time escaping.

It seemed not a single living Thornfield had stuck around, and Aurora didn't blame them. She hadn't been the only coven member longing for freedom. Or vengeance, as evidenced by the dead bodies of Stan's entire advisory panel, as well as the man himself and Aurora's mother.

Maybe witnessing her relatives' gruesome end would have hurt more if they hadn't buried her, knowing she'd suffocate when she returned to her body. As it was, Aurora didn't want to spare any more feeling for them than they'd spared her.

The humans were long gone. Well, not all the humans, Aurora noted. Gia's mobster brother still hovered awkwardly along the periphery. Aurora couldn't tell if Gia was too dazed to notice or was simply ignoring him.

Aurora wouldn't blame her if she were.

"Before we go, I'd like to ask him some questions." Aurora pointed to Marc.

Gia blinked at her brother. She seemed exhausted—no, dead on her feet. Being covered in dirt and blood didn't help. Aurora was sure she looked just as bad. As one might expect after crawling from a grave and then fighting for your life.

"That's probably a good idea." Gia sighed and called out to him. "What are you still doing here, Marc?"

He hurried over like he'd been waiting for permission. Blood splatters stained his fancy suit, a pained expression on his face. "I wanted to know what you're going to do now."

"None of your business."

Marc flinched.

"What are you doing here in the first place?" Aurora asked before he could collect himself. "How did Franco find Gia?"

Marc ran a nervous hand through his hair. "Father suspected Gia might come to Shearwater Landing."

Aurora had meant here at the compound, not in the city, but she let him continue.

"Once Father's witch was able to track you successfully, Gia, he knew he'd been right. You found your link to the Shearwater Landing witches. Father had reached out to this coven before"—he waved a hand vaguely, indicating the destroyed compound—"about an unrelated alliance, but the Thornfields weren't interested. He made another offer after you ran, and must have said something right because they agreed immediately."

Aurora rolled her eyes. "More like Stan's scheme with the Nightingales fell through, and he was desperate."

"Sure, whatever. I don't know the details." Marc scowled, barely averting his attention from his sister.

"Father agreed to ally with the Thornfields if they helped us bring you home. He was busy for the last few days meeting with the coven leader behind closed doors while witches and Salvator tracked you and kept tabs. But Gia, he wasn't a...a *vampire*."

Marc might not know the details, but Aurora suspected Trey had been involved. He'd never been there for her soul or the Lockwoods at all.

"He was a vampire," Gia said curtly. "He's been messing with my mind since I was a child. I had to get someone to undo his hypnosis. I saw him drink blood in the memories he erased. The fact that he erased my memory at all is evidence enough. Even if you didn't know before, come on, Marc, open your eyes. Franco could have hypnotized you to believe he was mortal and that you'd inherit his empire."

"But—"

"Didn't you see his eyes glowing? He wasn't human, and he wasn't a witch, or why would he need me to use magic?"

Marc inspected his surroundings, as if he might find answers in the ashes. "You're right about the magic. Okay. But

I'm so confused. Why am I remembering things differently all of a sudden?"

"Differently how?" Aurora asked.

"Now that I think about it, I *have* seen Father's eyes glow before, but if you'd asked me this morning, I'd have sworn against it. Everything in my past feels weird. Contradictory. I don't understand."

Surprise widened Gia's eyes, and the silence stretched, strained between the siblings.

Aurora spoke up hesitantly. "If Franco hypnotized you, now that he's dead, his hold will fade and reveal the truth. Your past might seem muddled if he covered up more than his vampirism."

Marc seemed to deflate. "Fuck. Okay. Do you think... Could he have *made* me follow him all this time? I remember believing him and wanting to be his heir, but it feels strange now. Like a dream."

Gia's expression crumpled. "He could have forced you. Oh my god, Marc. I never thought. Not even after I realized what he'd done to me."

Aurora hoped Marc had been under a thrall. There was a huge difference between Marc willingly following his father and being kept under a vampire's spell. "If you hurry and check now, a vampire might still detect the fading mind alterations. Then we'll know for sure."

Even if it was too late to see the evidence, Marc would know as his true memories surfaced. But Aurora had a feeling Gia would need solid proof to ever trust her brother again, and she wouldn't mind the confirmation herself.

Marc only seemed more lost than ever. "I'm sorry, Gia. About Ma." His voice broke, and his eyes turned glassy.

She regarded him with increased sadness. "Me too."

"That's what feels the most strange. I swear, I'd never..." He choked on a sob.

Gia's voice was thick with emotion. "I hope that's true. We'll ask Viv to look at your memory. Okay?" She turned and walked away, like she couldn't bear to face him a moment longer.

Aurora followed, leaving Marc behind. She caught Viv's eye, where she hovered near Sam and the other Lockwoods, and pointed at Marc.

With Viv's enhanced hearing, she'd likely heard their conversation, and sure enough, the vampire smirked and sauntered over to Marc without question.

"Do you think hypnosis is really the reason Marc stood by Franco?" Gia asked. "Do you think he forced Marc to stay at his side? To not care he'd killed our mother?"

"It's possible. And unless Marc is an excellent actor who actually knows everything about vampires, I'd say he's behaving exactly like someone coming out of hypnosis." He seemed like a completely different man than the one who'd accosted Gia on the street earlier.

"God, I hope you're right." A tear traced the curve of Gia's cheek. "Then at least one person in my life wasn't totally awful."

Aurora wrapped an arm around Gia. "Viv will sort him out and let us know. But I think we should head home."

Gia slumped against her. "You're coming with me?"

"Of course." That had never been in question. "If there's one thing we need right now, it's each other."

AURORA STIRRED, waking from a deep sleep, her body loose and rested. Damnation, it was good to sleep again.

Her stomach twisted with hunger. Yesterday, they'd

returned to the condo, showered, and crawled into bed. Aurora couldn't have looked at food if she'd tried, but now, she was painfully aware of how long it had been since she'd eaten.

She rolled over in bed, finding Gia already awake and watching her with one hand tucked under her cheek. It was light outside, so she assumed they'd slept all night. The first of the sun's rays shone in, bringing out the gold highlights in Gia's dark hair.

"Hey." Aurora's voice came out thick with sleep. "How are you doing?"

"Not bad. Sorry if I woke you."

"I'm not. I slept like a rock."

Gia smiled. "You obviously needed it."

"And you?" Gia seemed tired. How long had she been lying awake?

Her smile faded. "I had too many dreams. My mind's overloaded, and I'd say I'm worried about getting a migraine, except they were never real."

"The pain was real."

"Yeah, but it's still strange to wake up and remember everything I used to know was a lie." Gia scooted closer. "How are you doing?"

"I'm glad it's over." It would take a long time to process everything that happened to the Thornfields, especially her mother and uncle, but at the moment, the weight that had been lifted overshadowed everything else.

Gia reached for Aurora's hand. "I'm glad too. I didn't want you looking over your shoulder all your life, wondering if they'd come after you once you escaped."

Aurora had to admit, knowing the Thornfields wouldn't come calling was as big a relief as being free of the binding. "What about you? Will you have to worry about your father's men?"

Gia's lip curled. "I don't think so. Why bother with me when they can return to Ashton Lakes and fight over who's the new head of the organization? Besides, I don't think any of them are bullheaded enough to come for me after yesterday."

Unease washed away Aurora's relief. "You think?"

"I'm almost certain of it. Franco's death is an opportunity. His men were loyal to him, but not past death. Franco's power is gone. The only reason Salvator or the rest might come for me is if Marc takes over and orders them to. And it seems he won't be doing that." Her brow furrowed.

"What's that look?"

"Franco's men were loyal, but how much was hypnosis?" Gia sighed. "It doesn't matter. Point is, I'm not worried anyone will cause me trouble. I can kill them far easier than Franco was killed, and they know it."

Aurora's stomach twisted unpleasantly. "I'm sorry I channeled you to kill him."

Her eyes widened. "Why?"

"It's what Franco did to you, and I didn't ask if you were okay with killing him. We'd only discussed channeling to fight my coven."

"That's not true. I asked you to channel me because I trust you and the choices you make. If you hadn't made tough calls, Franco would have won."

"Maybe, but you can still feel conflicted about it."

Gia considered a moment longer before saying, "I wouldn't have made a single choice differently. I wanted him dead, and right now, I'm glad I was able to use the horrible things Franco forced me to do to beat him and help you. And I told Viv to finish him off. That was my call, not something you should feel responsible for."

"You're right," Aurora conceded.

"Maybe I shouldn't feel good about his death. I might see it differently one day, once time has passed. Who knows? Guilt could set in." She gave Aurora a vulnerable look.

Aurora scooted closer. "I'm not judging you for how you feel about it any more than you're judging me for how I handled things."

"I know you're not. But I want to make it clear: I'm never planning to use magic like that again."

"Me either. Life as a witch doesn't have to be bloody or full of terrible curses. I promise."

A small smile pulled at Gia's lips. "Thank god."

Aurora's stomach growled ridiculously loud, and she smashed her face into the pillow. Way to kill a heavy moment.

Gia laughed. "You must be starving."

Aurora turned, peeking out with one eye. "Not *starving*, but I could probably eat an entire breakfast buffet."

Gia's laugh deepened. "Let me see what I can do about that."

TWENTY-SIX

GIA

Gia and Aurora went to a café along the riverfront. Had Gia known the riverfront was so close to her condo? Had she even known a river ran through this neighborhood? No and no. But she forgave herself for not exploring until now.

Not having to look over your shoulder changed everything. Gia meant what she'd said about not being worried about Franco's men. She had no interest in taking over Franco's empire, so they had no reason to come for her, even if they were foolish enough to go against the very weapon Franco had used to intimidate everyone around him. Marc could take over if he wanted.

A pang settled in Gia's gut at the thought of her brother. Would he return to Ashton Lakes?

Viv had confirmed his mind had been altered. Not as extensively as Gia's, but there had been a tangle of commands and manipulations spanning fifteen years—as long as Franco had been a vampire.

Gia would have to catch up with Marc and see what he wanted to do now that he was free, but not today. The sun was heating up, and Gia was on her second coffee, Aurora on her third as she worked on a second plate of pancakes.

Nothing should interrupt such perfection.

Aurora had another bite. "I think I might pop, but it'll be worth it."

Gia smiled like a smitten fool. She couldn't get over how vibrant Aurora was. She'd been lovely as a ghost, but the full color, solid version of Aurora was magnificent.

Her hair was a sandy blonde, her cheeks a soft pink, and her nose dotted with freckles. She moved differently, too, no longer eerily graceful, and all the more alluring for it.

She was more alive than any person Gia had ever met. If they weren't in public, she didn't think she could resist pulling Aurora close and exploring every inch of her soft skin.

Would Aurora like that? They were no longer stuck together. How much would things between them change? Old worries lurked in Gia's mind. Sure, she'd passed the *does she like me the way I like her* hurdle, but that was the most basic assessment of compatibility.

They'd been through Hell together. Maybe that was the extent of their connection. Aurora had seen too much of Gia. Things Gia would have preferred a girlfriend not witness.

"You're thinking hard," Aurora said, setting her fork aside.

"I can't help it. I overthink most of the time." She always had.

"Does talking about whatever's on your mind help?"

Gia shifted in her seat. "I don't know. I don't usually share."

Aurora gave her the softest look. "I noticed. Don't worry, I get that. I didn't talk to people before I met Lilly and the other Lockwoods."

Something relaxed deep in Gia's soul. She'd forgotten how well Aurora understood her. There was far more between them than surviving yesterday's battles.

Gia could talk to Aurora. After everything, what was there

to be afraid of? "Maybe it's wrong to be worrying about this right now, but I was thinking about us."

"It's not wrong at all." Aurora grinned. "What's worrying you about us?"

Gia huffed, feeling ridiculous and embarrassed, and a whole bunch of other uncomfortable things. "I was wondering if you want to date me or if this was only in the moment. And now the moment is over."

Aurora reached across the table, and Gia offered her hand. Aurora clasped it. "Didn't I make myself clear yesterday?"

Gia's face heated. God, their graveside kiss had turned her inside out. "A girl can still overthink."

"True. So, let me be crystal clear. I want a relationship with you. We can go slow with dating if that's what feels right, but I don't want casual. I want to *know you,* Gia. And I want to show you who I am when I'm not floating around obsessing about my family and my past."

Gia squeezed Aurora's fingers. "Me too. I don't want to hold back anymore."

"Do you normally?"

She nodded. "It feels so inconsequential now. All my fear and uncertainties were such a waste. I let my family get in my head, and it wasn't the hypnosis."

Aurora's brow furrowed. "What were you afraid of?"

"Being dependent on Franco and my brother. I bought into how they treated me, and I wish I hadn't, but I can't blame them for everything. I held myself back when it had nothing to do with them. There was this girl, Tessa, and if I'd gone for it—took a chance—at least it wouldn't have been so drawn out."

"Was she your girlfriend?"

Gia almost laughed. "No. She's straight. I've never had a girlfriend." She hesitated. "Is that a dealbreaker?"

Aurora laughed, the sound bright and full of depth. "Are

you serious?" She rolled her eyes. "Yes, after you pulled me from my literal grave, your lack of dating experience is the deal-breaker."

"Shut up," Gia muttered without heat, fighting a smile.

Aurora leaned farther across the table. "Seriously. I don't mind." A sly smile curved her lush lips. "In fact, I like knowing I'll be the one introduce you to the wonders of sapphic life."

Gia's face flamed, her chest aching. "I wouldn't want it to be anyone other than you."

∼

AURORA TOOK her home along the scenic route, following the riverwalk and passing a bunch of shops, bars, and restaurants. Of all the places in the world for Gia to have landed, she was liking Shearwater Landing, and this neighborhood in particular. Franco and Marc would have called it run-down, but Gia found it charming.

She and Aurora reached home, the theater looming silently across the street. Gia imagined it open, lights glowing, and the marquee packed with show times.

A light flutter filled her chest.

"Well, look who it is," a familiar voice said, and Gia suppressed a sigh.

"Viv. You always seem to be lurking nearby."

The vampire smirked, showing the barest hint of fang. "Happens when you're neighbors."

"How's your application to join the Lockwoods going?" Aurora asked her.

Viv shrugged. "Pending. Figured I'd give the coven a break after yesterday before following up. No rush."

Gia wondered if vampires were ever in a rush, given their

unending lives. "Thanks for your help, in case I forgot to say it." The ride into the city was a blur, to say the least.

"Anytime." Viv swung what appeared to be a gym bag over her shoulder. "See you witches later." She sauntered away, whistling merrily.

"She's kind of..." Gia frowned. "Not creepy, but I don't know...off somehow."

"Vicious?" Aurora suggested.

"Definitely." Gia entered the building code, and they headed up the stairs. "Is that a vampire thing?"

"I don't know many vampires. No one outside the Lockwood Coven other than Viv. Usually, witches and vampires stick to separate covens. The Lockwoods are unique in that way."

"Does she fit in with the coven?" For the first time, Gia wondered how they decided which new members to accept. Was it like applying for a job or to join an exclusive club?

"I can see Viv fitting in as long as her willingness to shed blood is restricted to helping people, rather than for the sake of it."

Gia shuddered. "I guess we'll see."

Aurora broke into a blinding smile. "*We* certainly will."

Gia had no idea why Aurora said it like that, or why it seemed to make her so happy, but Gia would take it. Aurora's smile was the most gorgeous thing she'd ever seen.

They arrived at Gia's landing and pulled up short. Lilly stood outside the door.

"Lil!" Aurora rushed forward and the two embraced. "How'd you get in here?"

"Viv let me in. I texted," she added to Gia.

"I left my phone inside." She hadn't charged it yesterday, and it had died.

"I figured there was a reason you weren't answering, but I

couldn't stand sitting around waiting to hear from you. I needed to see you both with my own eyes."

"No problem." Gia quickly let them inside.

"We're having a coven meeting tomorrow," Lilly said, collapsing on the couch with Aurora. "No pressure to come, but you're both invited. Oh, and you're officially in, Aurora."

Aurora beckoned Gia closer, and she sat on the arm of the couch. Aurora immediately hugged her around the waist. "Glad they didn't decide I was too much trouble."

Lilly glared. "Don't even joke. If the Lockwoods stopped helping people like you, I'd leave. Besides, the elders agree that your link to us brought you to the theater."

Aurora sat straighter, her arm tightening around Gia. "Really?"

Lilly nodded. "You were a soul. Your most pure self, driven by your most true connections. You'd accepted us, and we'd accepted you, even if Edward hadn't finalized the coven documents. Connections like that mean something."

The idea gave Gia a giddy feeling. Personal connections held their own kind of power. Something that couldn't be forced or restricted. If that wasn't magic, Gia didn't know what was.

Aurora seemed deep in thought for a moment. "Getting trapped in the theater ended up being a good thing," she said eventually. "If I hadn't been pulled away and returned to my body immediately, I'd have realized my spell had failed and been trapped. No one would have known I was about to be married off, and I might never have gotten out."

Lilly's smile disappeared. "It seems like it happened this way for a reason."

Gia liked the idea of things happening for a reason. It was almost as if she'd shown up in Shearwater Landing for the purpose of helping Aurora. "Why do you think you got stuck with me if the Lockwoods pulled you to the theater?"

Before Aurora could open her mouth, Lilly chuckled. "Isn't it obvious?" She gestured between them, like her point was proven.

Gia's heart skipped. It was what she'd been thinking. "But Aurora and I couldn't have had a connection then. We didn't know each other when I walked into the theater." She glanced at Aurora. "I didn't even believe you were real."

"I won't say it's a fated connection between our souls." Aurora laughed at the prospect. "As far as I know, that kind of thing doesn't exist. But I also don't believe it's a coincidence my soul wouldn't leave your side."

Gia couldn't find it in herself to argue. "I like the sound of our souls being drawn together."

It was easy to believe they were meant for each other. No one else would understand Gia the way Aurora did. No one would make her feel safe enough to open up so completely. And with everything out of the way, they could enjoy each other. Enjoy life. Make it whatever they wanted it to be.

"I'm going to keep the theater," Gia said as if the others had been waiting impatiently for her decision, even though they hadn't even brought it up. "I want to open it again. Get shows running and start up the old movie screenings. Who in the coven should I talk to?"

Lilly clapped her hands together. "I'll give Maya your number."

Aurora's smile was soft. "Are you sure you want to keep it? You can do anything you want. Whatever you dreamed of. The coven can look after Spotlight for you."

Lilly nodded. "That's totally an option."

Gia's smile grew wider. "I don't have any unrealized dreams weighing me down. I want to be a part of the coven. Be a part of a group that helps people. Have a community. And if running the theater turns out not to be for me, I'll figure something out. After I give it a try."

"I'll help." Aurora squeezed her tight.

Gia ran a hand through Aurora's hair, treasuring each silken strand. "Is that what you want to do?"

"For now." Aurora's gaze turned distant. "I want to work within the coven. Help out. I've never thought about a career before, and I don't think there's anything I'd like to do in the human world, but who knows? Maybe I'll want to open a coffee shop or something." She laughed.

Lilly stayed for hours, catching Gia up on all things Lockwood. Gia had hoped to have time alone with Aurora, but she didn't begrudge Lilly's presence. Making friends within the coven was something she was looking forward to almost as much as going on her first official date.

And Lilly was far more likeable than Viv.

Lilly had brought a bag with her laptop, and after they'd exhausted the coven gossip, she suggested they watch a movie.

"Sounds perfect." Gia heaved herself off the couch. "Let me close the curtain."

"I might fall asleep," Aurora warned. She'd already curled beneath a blanket and didn't look like she'd be moving any time soon.

Lilly clicked around on the computer. "Hmm, relaxing vibes, let's see..."

Gia grabbed the curtain and froze. Marc was standing outside on the sidewalk.

"What is it?" Aurora sat up, fully alert.

"It's my brother."

She hurried to Gia's side, their arms brushing. "Do you want to talk to him?"

"Is it safe?" Lilly asked.

"I'm not worried about Marc. I need to find out exactly

what Franco did to his mind. The fact he hasn't fled the city is surprising." She'd guessed he'd be on a flight to Ashton Lakes. "I'm going to go talk to him."

Aurora grabbed her hand. "Want me to come?"

"I might get more out of him by myself, but you can keep an eye on me from the window if you're worried."

Aurora pulled the curtain as far open as it would go. "Oh, I will be. I know he was hypnotized, but I don't trust him yet."

Gia leaned in and brushed a quick kiss across Aurora's lips. "Thanks for looking out for me. I'll be back soon."

Aurora chased her retreating lips. "I'm counting on it."

As soon as Gia exited the building, Marc caught sight of her and raised his hands in surrender. "Gia, I just want to talk."

"I know, Marc. Relax."

He was more casually dressed than she'd seen him in years, wearing jeans, a hoodie, a baseball cap turned backward, and not a single piece of jewelry. "Your vampire friend told you my mind was messed up, right?"

"She's not exactly a friend, but yeah."

"I never would have stood by him if he hadn't forced me," Marc said in a rush. "I swear. Not after I figured out he'd killed Ma."

Gia wanted to weep with relief, but she held it together. "Why didn't he erase the memory of what he'd done, like he did with me?"

Marc shrugged, looking hopelessly lost. "He made me into the man he wanted, altering anything he didn't like. Ordering me to believe him. To buy into his thinking. It's fucked. I can remember all his commands now. All the times I disagreed or argued with him, and he smoothed it over so I'd forget. And the worst thing is, after a while, he didn't have to do that anymore. It's like he smashed me into a mold, and eventually, I gave in."

Gia's heart ached. "Marc..."

"I know." Marc adjusted his hat nervously. "For years, I held all these beliefs, thinking they were genuinely mine, and they weren't. Even the ones like Ma that I fought the hardest, he eventually figured out how to force me to accept."

"Jesus Christ." Gia patted his shoulder.

His posture relaxed almost imperceptibly. "I don't know if I'd have wanted to inherit his empire any more than you did if he hadn't forced me. I don't think any of it was me. After fifteen years of this shit, I don't know who I am."

"Oh, Marc, I'm so sorry."

He reached for her and hesitated. She pulled him into a hug. "No, I'm sorry for what he did to you, Gia. I'd never have accepted it if he hadn't forced me."

"I believe you." Gia pulled away, hardly recognizing the man before her. Who was her brother without his ambition? Without the Balzano legacy? "What are you going to do now?"

Marc glowered. "Fuck if I know. I can't go back."

"Who do you think will take over?"

"Salvator will try, and then the Russians will rip him to shreds. Or someone else will. Maybe Salvator will win. I couldn't care less as long as I never see any of them again."

"My thoughts exactly."

They shared a strained smile.

Marc was right. Now that Franco and his supernatural influence were gone, the humans would fight it out and see who rose to the top. The winner didn't matter to Gia or Marc in the least.

"I'm going to stay here for a while," Marc said, looking down the road like he might find directions for the rest of his life on a street sign. "Maybe I should take some classes and see if I have any skills beyond being a dumbass."

"Hey, you aren't a dumbass. Neither of us can help what Franco hypnotized us to do."

"I suppose not." He sounded defeated.

"If Salvator or anyone comes looking for you, let me know."

Marc smiled fully, in a way she hadn't seen since they were kids. "Thanks, G. You're the best sister."

She rolled her eyes. "Your only sister."

He shoved his hands in his pockets. "What are you going to do? Are you staying here?"

She nodded, gesturing across the street. "I'm going to reopen the theater my Aunt Susan left me. Hey"—she playfully smacked his shoulder—"if I can't find enough employees, you can be an usher or a concession operator or something. In case you can't find a job."

Marc looked horrified by the idea. "Thanks…"

Gia laughed, shoving him again, like she used to do when they were young, and he grinned. "What? Is working in a theater not good enough for you?"

His cheeks reddened. "It's not that. Okay. Maybe a little. Damn, I need to adjust my world view."

More like rid himself of Franco's world view.

"Don't worry about it, Marc. You'll be fine. Let me know if you need anything. Seriously." She meant it, but prayed he didn't need a place to sleep.

"Thanks. I should be okay for now."

Gia smiled. "Glad to hear it."

The last thing she needed now that she had her first girlfriend was her brother crashing in her one-bedroom condo.

EPILOGUE

AURORA

Six months later.

It was opening night for Maya's latest production, and the Spotlight Theater was packed. While this was the coven headquarters, the shows and movie screenings had always been human-friendly. Not all the actors were witches, and the lighting and sound were done by human technicians. Aurora loved how the theater served as a place for the whole neighborhood, not only witches and vampires.

Covens like the Thornfields only succeeded in isolation, and Aurora would much rather hide her magic ability in public than be cut off from so much of the world. Living amongst human society made life brighter.

Gia found her at the bottom of the stairs. "The doors are shut."

The music swelled in the theater beyond. "You look excited."

Gia grinned, her cheeks flushed. "I am. I might not have acting or singing skills, but I love this."

"Yeah?" Aurora pulled her close. "Even with all the late nights and staffing drama."

Gia rolled her eyes. "I'd hardly call it drama."

In truth, the staff were great. Aurora had worked more closely with them when they'd first reopened for movie nights, but she was becoming less involved as time went on. She wasn't as enthusiastic about running the theater as Gia. Especially when it came to the business side. Aurora had quickly learned to avoid the office, and not because she'd once been trapped in there.

Gia, on the other hand, was all business, happily taking care of all the tasks that made Aurora's mind fog over. Aurora might not mind hiding magic sometimes, but human work wasn't for her.

Luckily, Gia had helped her settle on the perfect alternate career. The woman was full of brilliant ideas.

Gia glanced around the lobby. "I don't think there's anything else we need to do until intermission."

The staff did seem to have it covered. "Shall we wait it out in the office?"

"An excellent idea." Gia led her up the stairs and along the hall. "How was your class today?"

Aurora's stomach flipped. "I think it went well."

At Gia's suggestion, Aurora had started helping one of the coven elders teach magic lessons. After Aurora had taught her the magic basics, Gia had claimed she was a natural teacher.

While most witches were taught by their parents, family members, or tutors, Gia wasn't the only one to miss out and find themselves an adult in need of training. Working with children wasn't for Aurora, but she loved teaching adults, whether it was basic stuff or more complex theory. She was even helping run an advanced session on magical research, diving deep into counter spell construction. Picking things apart and building new spells stretched Aurora's mental legs in a way working in the theater simply hadn't.

She loved living in the human world, but magic needed to be her main endeavor.

"It only went well?" Gia asked as they reached the office, her teasing tone clear.

"Okay, it was great. I've got a bunch of reading to do before we test our latest theory, and the beginners did so well yesterday."

Gia beamed, shutting the door behind her and clicking the lock. "I love seeing you happy."

Aurora pressed her against the door. "Yeah, well, I love seeing *you* happy. You're glowing."

Gia's hands settled at her waist. "That's because I have something important to ask you."

"Oh?" Aurora brushed Gia's hair off her forehead, butterflies swarming her chest.

Gia's hands tightened. "Will you move in with me?"

Aurora crushed her into a kiss, their mouths meeting in a rush, bodies pressed tight. "I'd love to."

She'd been living with Lilly and her other roommates, and while it was fun, Aurora was ready to settle into her relationship with Gia. She wanted to marry this woman. Raise beautiful fur-babies with her. See musicals and ballets and whatever else Maya decided to produce for the Spotlight stage. She wanted to watch old movies in the balcony, and kiss in the street.

She wanted everything with Gia. It was a life Aurora feared she'd never have, and now that it was hers, she and Gia were going to make the most of it. Nothing held back.

Vengeance had been sweet, but this was sweeter.

The End

Need more of Aurora and Gia? Join my newsletter for a free bonus scene.

What's next for the Lockwood Coven? Viv's story, *Her Deadly Bite,* is coming soon.

Want to know a secret? Harper Nightingale was just as desperate to get out of the betrothal and escape his coven as Aurora. Read his story in *Demon's Mate.*

I hoped you enjoyed Gia and Aurora's story.

Reviews are invaluable to authors. Please consider leaving a review for *Her Ghostly Embrace* on your favorite review site or the site where you purchased this book to help others find magical books they'll love.

ACKNOWLEDGMENTS

Thank you, dear reader, for coming on this wild ghostly ride with me. This book is close to my heart. I've been thinking about it for years and being able to share it with you is the reason I keep writing.

Thank you to Laura, from Hummingbird Editing, for working with me on this story, catching my errors and making valuable suggestions, as well as chatting with me about all kinds of magical things, brainstorming taglines, and helping me remember tropes. It's always a blast.

Thank you Callie, from CJ Editing, for proofreading another Shearwater Landing book! It's been great working with you once again.

And thank you Jess, for the stunning cover art. You brought Aurora and Gia to life, surpassing my wildest dreams! Aurora's ghostly hair is everything I ever wanted.

Finally, thank you to TK for your eternal support. I hope you liked this one.

ABOUT THE AUTHOR

Colette (she/they) is an author of queer paranormal romance novels living in New Zealand. Colette loves to write couples who take care of each other and show their soft sides in love, even when they're prickly in other facets of their lives. Sugar, spice, and magic are key ingredients in all of Colette's books.

Colette can be found on Instagram @colette_rivera and on Facebook under Colette Rivera Author. Colette can also be found on their website coletterivera.com where you can sign up to their newsletter for bonus epilogues and updates.

Shearwater Landing World:

Lovers of the Damned

Demon's Mate

Demon's Heart

Demon's Desire

Devil's Mate

Bound in Blood

His Eternal Temptation

Shearwater Landing Shorts

I Think I Found a Vampire

More Magical Worlds:

Moonlight Falls

The Fall of Elijah Gray

The Seduction of James Gray

The Cursed Sebastian Storm

The Heart of Moonlight Falls

Love & Magic

Give a Witch a Chance

Keep Your Witches Close

One Wicked Night

Witch Boyfriend Wanted

www.ingramcontent.com/pod-product-compliance
Lightning Source LLC
Chambersburg PA
CBHW030907060726
47591CB00005B/1453